# OLLIE'S LOST

# OLLIE'S LOST

## SHREY SAHJWANI

PARTRIDGE
A Penguin Random House Company

**To order additional copies of this book, contact**
Partridge India
000 800 10062 62
www.partridgepublishing.com/india
orders.india@partridgepublishing.com

# ONE

## TRICK OF THE TRADE

U niversal Trade Towers—a marvellous skyscraper made entirely of glass! Beams of sunlight shine off the surface of the glass, thinning out as they reach the lower floors. This building was the pinnacle of architectural ingenuity. If you didn't believe me, you could just ask the rest of the residents of Toronto; they'd agree in a heartbeat. Everyone who passed by it was possessed by an urge to go inside the building, just because it was such a well-known landmark. I never thought in a million years I'd be sitting in a waiting room at the top of it, on the sixty-ninth floor.

I don't like being made to wait for too long, but I'm not an overly impatient sort of guy either. I had been waiting to be called in to a situation, which, to me, could only be described as '*hell.*' To my left, there are half a dozen people. Two of them were teenagers sitting amongst themselves. I could tell they were young by how they looked. One had curly orange hair and wore spectacles. What he lacked in facial hair he made up for with acne; the other, a young Asian boy who had hair so slick from oil that you could use the follicles as a mirror. To their side sat a man who looked about my age. He was far better dressed than I was. He made me nervous and uncomfortable because the moment I saw him, I was certain he was here for the same job as I was, and to top it all, he came better prepared. *Asshole!* Just because he wore a suit to a job interview, he'd be a more suitable prospect for the job! I began doubting my choice of attire for the interview. When I woke up this morning, I rummaged through my wardrobe for what seemed like hours. Finally, I went with my favourite fitted tan and white striped shirt with the sky blue tie that my girlfriend picked out. I suddenly felt embarrassed because the tie must have made me look tremendously *douchey* (for lack of a better word . . .) I don't always wear ties to job interviews, but my

1

girlfriend suggested that this particular shade of sky blue brought out my eyes. I never saw what made her jump to that conclusion, seeing as how my eyes are grey and not a deep blue. I didn't go with my usual ruffled up hairstyle. Today, specifically for this job interview, I parted my thin blond hair to the side. I didn't look twenty-six today; I looked like a thirty-year-old. The ad in the paper said they were looking for a young marketing professional. *Damn it, Ollie!* How could I manage to look like such a tool? I should've worn a suit like the other guy!

I sat there staring at the man in the suit, twiddling my thumbs, and trying to subdue thoughts of throttling this man who, I concluded, was clearly overdressed for this interview. Humouring my homicidal tendencies, I thought up a convenient place to do it. I couldn't have murdered him here in the crowded waiting room, and the door that led to the main office in front of us had restricted access to people that had a key card in their possession. If this murder were to go down, it would have to have been in the visitors' bathroom to my right. Maybe if I dunked him in the toilet headfirst, the police would write it off as an accident. Just as I came up with the five hundred and fifth method of getting rid of him, a man who appeared to be in his late thirties walked out the main door of the office into the visiting room filled with hopeful candidates. I sat back straight in my chair. Of course I wanted to make a good first impression if this was the guy that would be interviewing me. The man smiled and steered his large frame in my direction; his eyes met mine but only momentarily. He was not here to see me.

He took a few steps to my left and greeted the man in the suit. They exchanged handshakes and hugs and then made their way to the large glass door at the end of the hallway towards the elevator.

In the Universal Trade Towers building, or the UTT as the locals say, there's the office of a firm that provides Public Relations and Marketing strategies to media companies called *The Trick of the Trade*. It had been number one in Toronto in the field for as long as I could remember. I thought about why no other name stuck out as much as The Trick of the Trade, and it dawned on me that the key to this business was its image. Holding office space in the most expensive and elite building of the city was a business card in its own right. The Trick of the Trade was owned by Bill Jacoby, a man whose name opened many doors for many people. It's awfully poetic that he's also the man who would be capable of slamming doors shut on people's careers. He's quite a flashy dresser. Not that I'd ever seen him before in person, but he's a socialite and is famous for being all over the news for something or the other. His style sensibilities were prominent all over the office I was in, with a long corridor leading into the office and spotless wooden floors which were polished regularly, weekly, by the looks of it. Marble tables for receptionists and secretaries in the waiting room and plush white leather couches on the sides at the tip of the entrance door. Everything about this place screamed glamour, with the exception of my tan shirt and sky blue tie, *What was I thinking when I came here looking like this?*

I still had hope, and I was not ready to part with it just yet. The man in the suit had left the building with another employee, which meant I was back in the running to getting the job of my dreams! Well, it wasn't really what I envisioned myself doing. If you *asked six-year-old me* what I'd be doing twenty years from now, I'd say something dreamy and inspirational like, 'I want to be an astronaut!' or 'I want to help animals, so I'll become a vet!' Never would the words *Oliver Turner, Campaign Strategist,* escape my lips.

'Turner, Oliver Turner,' announced a blonde woman wearing a pink shirt tucked into something. (It looked like it was tucked into something. I mean from where I was sitting, she looked like a floating head. The grand marble desk she was sitting at covered up her entire lower body and most of her upper body.) She glanced over at me, and the others in the waiting room, awaiting a response. I stood up and walked up to the receptionist's table. 'That's me,' I said, clearing my throat.

'Mister Astiff will see you now,' she said as she pressed a shiny red button on a panel button on a panel filled with different-coloured switches embedded on the desk. The second she pressed it, the large glass doors behind her opened, almost as if it were magic. *Say what you will about him, this Bill Jacoby fellow knows how to make an office look grand.*

'Ah, hell at last,' I said under my breath.

'It's not that bad,' said a man who looked, surprisingly, a lot like me. In fact, he was even wearing the same shirt as I was. *Maybe that's what I'll look like twenty years from now.* He seemed like a hard-working person and looked as though he worked a small sales job. He probably made about half as much as I was going to ask for. I thought this guy was easy-going, because he dressed like me so maybe he had the attitude to match.

'Did I say that out loud? I . . . I'm so sorry. It's just that job interviews make me nervous. I'm supposed to meet a guy. He's probably some big shot who's going to pay no attention to what I have to say anyway. But you probably know all about corporate douche bags,' I said, smiling coyly.

He let out a chuckle and said, 'This way.' I followed him through the office, which was sprawling with life and energy. Everyone in the cubicles, clustered up in the centre of the office space, appeared to be busy with something or the other. Along the sides of the cubicles were medium-sized glass cabins. They had nameplates screwed on metal plates on the doors. I managed to glance at some of the designations in passing, *Sr. Executive, VP Creative, Programme's Head, Sr. Client Servicing.* All the cabins had windows with panoramic views of the Toronto Skyline.

Towards the end of the hall, there was a slightly bigger cabin in the corner. This cabin wasn't like the other cabins. The curtains were drawn, sealing any remnants of light away, casting a shadow of darkness all around it. The nameplate on the door read *Robert Astiff, VP Human Resources/Client Servicing.*

'Wow, this guy's such a weirdo! Why does he like the darkness so much?' I questioned.

The aging man in front of me chuckled again. *He never really says much, does he?* I wondered. He opened the door and walked inside. I followed him. He walked behind the desk and took a seat.

'So, Oliver, tell me about yourself.'

'Wait a minute! You're Mister Astiff?' I asked, hoping that he'd say no.

He laughed again. 'The honesty that you brought to the table was . . .' he paused, thinking of the right word.

4

'Retarded,' I said, finishing his sentence for him.

'Woah! Not going for politically correct, are we? I was thinking more on the lines of refreshing . . . but let's go with that!' he quipped.

'I'm so sorry, I had no idea!' I said, feeling the need to salvage any hopes of finishing this interview in one piece.

'Relax, you remind me a lot of myself when I was younger,' he said.

I was amazed at how like-minded we were about that. He saw pieces of his youth in me, and I saw my future in him. *Oh god, no! I called him a corporate douche bag and a weirdo! I'm doomed!*

'Look, I know how interviews go. I've been on both sides of them many times in my life. There's no right way to go about these things.' His tone was reassuring, but I sensed that there was more to it than that. He probably just wanted to get this done with quickly so he could have a laugh with his friends over this interview that went horribly wrong right off the bat.

'I like your shirt,' I said, trying to get him to forget all the cheap shots I took at him, unknowingly, earlier on.

He laughed. At this point, I began thinking that he'd laugh at anything. 'Well, I guess I should say the same to you. My wife picked this out for me. What's your excuse?' he asked.

'Girlfriend,' I said. We both giggled about it for a while before proceeding with the interview.

'My name is Oliver Turner. I'm twenty-six years old. I've been in the business for eight years now. I live here in Downtown Toronto with my girlfriend for four years,' I said, pausing not knowing whether to carry on or give him a chance to ask another question.

'Don't tell me . . . you're going to propose soon?' he asked.

'How did you . . . ' I was baffled at how he knew that. Until he suggested it, even I wasn't sure of whether or not I was going to go through with it.

'Like I said, you remind me of myself when I was younger,' he said while tapping his pen on a sheet that listed my credentials. I, in turn, smiled at him. I'd often been proven wrong every time I was quick to judge someone. By the looks of things, I was right to have liked this guy the second I spoke to him. 'How much are you looking for, financially, from us?' he added.

'$60,000 a year,' I said, stoic.

'When can you start?' he said, equally emotionless.

'How about right now?' Perhaps I was too keen to answer that question. Why did I seem so eager? Did I misread that question? Maybe he was only asking out of curiosity. There was no sign of give in his voice that should have led me to believe that he was offering me the job.

He smiled and looked into my eyes. He went on to say, 'You've got balls, kid. I'll give you that.' He placed the sheet with my name on top of it into a folder and closed it. 'See you on Monday,' he said.

'You're fucking with me, right?' I said, in disbelief. *I had gotten the job!*

For what seemed like the millionth time, he laughed and said, 'Yes. But I must warn you, the others don't take kindly to profanity in the workplace.'

'Shit . . . I mean . . . Crap. I'm sorry. I'll wash my mouth out with soap when I get home,' I said, standing up to shake his hand.

He held my hand in his and said, 'Great fucking idea, kid!' as the two of us laughed out loud.

I walked out of the building and walked across the street, staring up at the building in the general direction of the sixty-ninth floor.

*My name is Oliver Turner. I'm twenty-six years old, and I work for The Trick of the Trade in the UTT.*

I was going to have to keep reassuring myself that this was true. The more I said it the more I began to believe it. There was still a ton of doubts in my mind as to what Robert saw in me. Why did he give me the job after I fumbled the whole time? For whatever reason, he liked me and now I had a job.

On my way home, I stopped at a jewellery store called *Jade*. The shop was lit with green-tinted chandeliers, which reflected their light off the black granite flooring. Even the shop itself looked like a jewel from the outside. On the inside, it was a feast for the senses. I walked over to a man dressed in all black standing behind the glass showcase, featuring engagement rings. I looked for one that caught my attention most. It was a matter of seconds before my eyes were fixated on a beautiful princess cut engagement ring. *That's the one I'm getting.*

Within minutes, the ring had been purchased and put into a nice blue box made of velvet. I put the box in my trouser pocket and made my way home to my girlfriend.

A successful job interview and a marriage proposal: Jenna won't know what hit her!

# TWO

## UNCLE MARIO

I had been dating Jenna since the day I turned twenty-two. We were friends before that day, through a long line of mutual friends. We weren't really close, but we weren't mere acquaintances either. The idea of Jenna and me came about from something a friend of mine said.

It was 26 April, the eve of my birthday, a night I would never forget. My friend Mathew was throwing a party for me at his new apartment. He had invited a bunch of people and had made all the arrangements without letting me lift a finger. Mathew, or Matt as his close friends called him, and I went a long way back. In high school, he was the sort of kid that would be bullied more often than not. Scrawny little guy, all of four feet nothing, black hair slickly parted to the side and he even had braces back then. Needless to say, he wasn't Mister Popular. Back then, I was a lot taller, and in retrospect, I realised I was a better-looking guy too because a handful of the more popular girls in school were vying for my favour. The bullies were in the middle of pulling Matt's underpants over his head when I told them to quit it and take a walk. They argued for a while and eventually gave up and went about doing their business elsewhere. I didn't know what it was that encouraged me to stop them; perhaps I intervened because I felt sorry for him. Well, whatever it was that inspired that act was responsible for me finding a best friend in him today. Today, Matt stands just over six feet tall, towering over pretty much everyone in the same room as him, even me by a couple of inches. Hours of dedication and perspiration at the gym had now made him the object of every woman's desire. His thick black hair was always ruffled up, systematically making it look as though he had just gotten out of bed at any point in the day. When he smiled, a dimple would grace his left cheek and his light brown eyes would light up. If I didn't have Jenna in my life, I'd probably be jealous of him. That was four years ago, and we had since lost touch. The last memory I have of him was how he was instrumental in helping me find Jenna.

Matt and I had been talking about all things work-related sitting on a couch, making business-related jokes for the amusement of the people around us at the time, not noticing what was going on around the rest of the house, filled with people who were there just for me. That was until Jenna walked in. She was wearing a silky green one-shoulder dress that barely reached her knees. Her strawberry blonde hair was left open and flowing, covering the backless portion of the dress. I stared at her shamelessly for a while, not caring about what she or anyone else thought at the time because who could blame me for looking at someone who looked as ravishing as her that night. After a few moments of gathering my thoughts, I walked up to her and said hello.

'Happy birthday!' she said as she hugged me. As I returned the hug, I caught a whiff of her perfume. It felt as though I had just dived head first into a strawberry patch and landed on the sweetest smelling lot. Her hair had a freshly shampooed smell, and everything about her just seemed to cause my heart to skip a beat every now and then. I thanked her and went back to my conversation with Matt after a friend of Jenna came and whisked her away into another room.

'You should hit that,' Matt said to me. I just sat there and nodded. The conversation around me continued, but I had tuned out completely. I'd occasionally pretend to pay attention to what was going on and smile politely when conversation was being made directly with me, but my eyes kept wandering around the room to find Jenna. Eventually, I'd had enough of pretending to care about everyone else in the world and excused myself. My absconding didn't ruffle any feathers because everyone thought I was just dragging the conversation down with my unwillingness to participate in it. I walked up to Jenna and asked her if she wanted to go somewhere more private. She was confused, but she obliged me anyway, with it being my birthday and all.

I walked outside the apartment with her and not knowing where to go ended up taking her to the roof. We sat there talking and laughing, gazing at stars and drinking a little alcohol I had smuggled from downstairs. I was beginning to like this girl. After a while, the two of us had gotten hungry. I decided to take her to a place I used to frequent a few kilometres north of Matt's Apartment in Sheppard's Avenue; *Uncle Mario's Pizza Place*. *Uncle Mario's* was a typically over the top Italian-themed restaurant: wooden furniture with picnic-styled park benches for seats and picnic tables covered with a red and white chequered tablecloth. The servers all wore shirts that were the same colours as the tablecloth with denim overalls and a hat with a big red M on the side. I went to middle school with a couple of guys that worked there. They were all happy to see me whenever I went in there. They'd even give me a discount from time to time.

Jenna loved the place from the second she stepped in. Who could blame her, when you walked into *Uncle Mario's, Uncle Mario* himself would greet you from behind the counter and you'd instantly become part of the family. The pizzas were great but not phenomenal enough to inspire multiple visits. The only reason everyone who ate at Mario's ate there was because no matter what mood you walked in with, you'd leave with a big smile on your face. That was my first date with Jenna; after which I walked her home.

'Would you like to come in for a bit?' she asked, fiddling with her keys atop her doorstep. I thought about my answer long and hard.

'Not tonight, sweetheart,' I said as I kissed her cheek. She looked disheartened, and I didn't like that. All I wanted was to not sabotage the promise of a relationship. I wanted this to mean more to her than just a one-night stand, the only way of guaranteeing that it happened to be so would be to deny the nightcap. 'Don't be sad. Let me make it up to you . . . Dinner tomorrow? I'm buying!' I said. This made her smile. She nodded her head as she headed to the door, opened it, and walked in.

Maybe it was because of those events that Jenna and I were at this stage in our relationship. Maybe it was because of that date at *Uncle Mario's* that I fell for her so hard. And maybe that was the reason I was here today, four years later: on the same table across the same person with whom I had that date. *Uncle Mario's* had a live band playing on odd nights of the week. I saw to it that tonight was one of those nights. The band in the background was doing what they do best: plucking different strings of different instruments and singing. There was no one to appreciate them but Jenna and myself. I hadn't arranged for that to happen; it was just a slow night. Uncle Mario had been instructed to keep sending wine to our table whenever the bottle was empty and to cue the band to walk up to our table and work their magic upon my signal.

Halfway through the meal, I looked over at Uncle Mario who was eagerly awaiting a signal that we hadn't devised yet. Several times I had spotted him lunging forward because he was unsure as to whether or not me scratching my brow was a signal or tapping my hands on the table meant to set off the fireworks. When the time came for him to be alerted, I looked at him and nodded. He acknowledged that as the signal and went ahead and signalled the band in the same way.

They approached our table and began to play a soft and deep romantic tune. I got out of my seat and got down on one knee in front of Jenna. She was taken by surprise, and it was quite evident. I shouldn't have been nervous, because even Uncle Mario knew what her answer was going to be, but I was. There's something about proposing to a woman that will set any man on edge. I knew that it was long overdue and that she would say yes no matter what, but I couldn't stop my hands from trembling with anxiety.

'Jenna . . . ' I said, calculating my next set of words because those would be the ones that she'd remember more than any I'd ever said in the past.

'Ollie!' she said, smiling as tears escaped her eyes.

'Will you marry me?' I barely finished the sentence before she sprang up and yelled, 'Yes!' I put the ring on her finger, and she pulled me up to my feet and kissed me. Uncle Mario and the rest of the staff at the restaurant clapped and cheered as the band went on to play more upbeat celebratory music.

Jenna was so elated. I had known for a while now that she had been expecting a proposal, and I didn't even mind it. My parents loved her, her parents loved me, and more importantly than all that, we loved each other. She immediately picked up the phone and called her mother, crying out of happiness. Seeing her so happy made me blush a little. I knew that she always had the power to make me immensely happy. Today, I finally had the chance to return the favour.

Doggy bag in hand, we walked home from *Uncle Mario's* as *soon to be Mr and Mrs Oliver Turner*. For the rest of the evening, we referred to each other as husband and wife. It hadn't sunk in yet, but my dream of marrying Jenna was finally shaping up to become a reality.

*My name is Oliver Turner. I'm twenty-six years old. I work at The Trick of the Trade in the UTT, engaged to be married to Jenna, my soulmate.*

At this point, it was clear that I was going to have to get used to telling myself what was real and what wasn't.

# THREE

## Breakfast in Bed

When I awoke the next morning, I leaped forward and checked Jenna's hand to see if the ring was still on her finger. *Yep, still there . . . I wasn't dreaming last night.* Jenna was asleep next to me in our peaceful bedroom in our recently acquired home. Jenna and I had decided to move in together a couple of years ago. She sold her apartment, and we used the money from that as a down payment on the mortgage. I was living on rent at the time and gave that place up. It was a logical decision because the property value went up significantly since then and thanks to the big down payment from Jenna, the mortgage was hardly alarming enough to cause sleepless nights.

You could tell just by looking around the place that it had a woman's influence. The furniture was posh and sophisticated. We had a glass dining table in the living room with four black leather chairs around it in the corner that was on the opposite side of the window. The chairs had stems of metal for legs. On the side closer to the window was a black leather couch in front of which was a small rectangular coffee table and makeshift magazine collection made of glass and black painted wood. The wall in front of the couch had a thirty-two-inch plasma TV mounted on it. We'd sometimes cuddle up on the couch and watch a movie, or sometimes even a rerun of a really old classic. On either side of the living room were entrances to bedrooms. Jenna and myself decided on getting a three-bedroom home because we liked the idea of having a spare room for whatever reason. The price wasn't too much more than a slightly smaller home in the same neighbourhood, so we thought that it would be the wiser choice.

When we just moved in, Jenna had taken control of the interiors. I had full faith in her abilities. She had just started up her own Interior Design firm after quitting her earlier job at *Les Designe;* a popular décor firm in the suburbs. She had a bunch of clients then, and it seems as though they were satisfied because they stayed on with her. I could not be more proud of my wife-to-be than I was now.

I decided that she deserved breakfast in bed just because of how pretty she looked when she was asleep. She slept with one arm under her pillow while she lay on her side. She was smiling; certainly she didn't know that she was. Her hair looked flawless, despite the long hours of tossing and turning. I knew she was doing that because she always ended up kicking me or pushing me into the wall in her sleep at odd hours of the night. I never told her anything about it because it was comforting to know that she was still there, and besides . . . whenever she does toss and turn a lot, I would automatically assume she's just having a nightmare and hold her close to me and kiss her cheek. That generally kept her still for enough time for me to fall back asleep.

I tiptoed out of the room, and when I got to the door, I glanced back towards the bed to see whether she was still asleep. *Score! She hadn't flinched.* I made my way through the living room to the kitchen. I put a black pan on the stove and poured a little bit of oil in it. I hadn't decided what I was going to make for her, but I was fairly certain that every dish in my repertoire of breakfast foods involved some amount of frying. I pulled out a couple of eggs from the grey cardboard box in the fridge and cracked them open into a bowl. I chopped up a tomato and some onions and sprinkled salt and pepper into the bowl. While I was whisking the eggs and other ingredients in the bowl, the oil in the pan began splattering. My kitchen know-how was limited, but even I knew that was my cue to pour the contents of the bowl into the pan. I watched as the eggs began to take the shape of the pan. I reached out for a wooden spoon on the tabletop and tried to flip the egg, but I was unsuccessful. *I hope she likes her eggs scrambled, because there's no way I can salvage this omelette.* A few moments later, the scrambled eggs were ready. I tried to make them look fancy on the plain white plate that I poured them into, but nothing says 'boring' quite like a plate, filled halfway with scrambled eggs and nothing else. I poured some more oil into the pan and began searching in the freezer. *Mmm . . . Bacon.* I pulled out a couple of strips that were stuck to each other because of the ice that had formed on them and tossed them into the pan, flipping them over and over, impatiently. After they became crispy and acquired the brownish tinge, I picked them off the pan with the wooden spatula I used to scramble my omelette and placed them neatly on the plate. I then pulled out a glass and wiped it clean and then began to fill it with orange juice. Breakfast was ready, and even though it may not have seemed like much, I was proud of my efforts.

I walked into the bedroom with the meal I had just prepared, marvelling at my creation up until the point where I was looming eerily over the Jenna. I placed the glass of juice on the white wooden bedside table and shook her until she woke up. I was as persistent as she was reluctant; eventually, she gave in and woke up. I placed the plate on her lap and said, 'Bon appétit.' She smiled and pulled my cheek close to her and kissed it. She filled up a fork with a mouthful of eggs and took a bite. 'Thank you,' she said, with her mouth full. I stood there and watched her eat her meal. Jenna would tell me how annoying I was when I'd do strange things like that. The truth is I never really knew when I begin doing them. Sometimes she'd be getting dressed and I'd stop what I was doing to look at her. The only time I stop looking is either when I'd realised that it may seem awkward if she caught my gaze or when she would tell me to cut it out.

'Mmm . . . Bacon,' she said as she took a bite of one of the strips in front of her.

'I know, right?' It amazed me that she and I were so alike in some ways but entirely different in others. We never liked the same food. We rarely share the same first opinions about new people that we're introduced to. I hate the books she loves, and she hates the books I love. We were like two pieces on the same puzzle: nothing like each other but somehow, when one piece was fixed to the other, it made sense.

She took only a fraction of the time to devour the food that it took me to make it. She gulped down the juice and put the glass on top of the plate and let them both sit on the table before going back into her sideways position on the bed. 'Thanks, honey,' she said to me as she turned her head away from me.

'You're kidding me, right?' I had spent the last twenty minutes or so catering to her every need and all she wanted to do was go back to sleep.

All I got in return was '*Thanks, honey.*' If only she could look into my mind for a moment to see how enraged this act was making me.

'Get back in bed. I want to cuddle.' She didn't turn her head back to say this to me.

'Okay. I'm in.'.

———◈———

I would lie in that bed with Jenna in my arms forever had it not have been for the constant ringing of my cell phone. Jenna began to stir and kicked my shin gently. 'Okay, okay! I'll get it,' I said whilst reluctantly stretching to the bedside table to get my phone. The bright blue light on the screen flashed 'MOM'. I hadn't even told her I had proposed to Jenna. I didn't even discuss the possibility with her, or anyone for that matter.

'Hello?' I said, trying not to sound like I had just woken up.

'Oliver J Turner! Why on Earth are you asleep at half past two in the afternoon?' my mother yelled.

Obviously, my attempt at fooling her had been unsuccessful. My mother was still yelling at me over the phone, but I wasn't listening because I was too engrossed in trying to get out of bed to go to the living room without waking Jenna. Somehow, I managed to get out of bed and walk into the living room.

'Mom . . .' I said, but my mother was still going on about how embarrassing it was to have a son that did nothing but sleep all day.

'When will you get your priorities right, Ollie?' my mother asked, seeming concerned.

'I got the job, mom!' I exclaimed.

'The one at the UTT? Oh my god, that's amazing news, honey! Congratulations!' she said.

'Oh and mom, Jenna and I are officially engaged now,' I added.

My mother wasn't the *shrieky* sort, but even someone as seasoned as her couldn't take news this big calmly. I couldn't tell what she was saying because amidst the shrieking and the crying, it all sounded like gibberish to me, but I knew that she was happy. My parents loved Jenna because they knew how happy she made me.

'M-Mom, please calm down . . . I can't understand a word you're saying.' I tried making sense of her last few sentences, but it was hopeless.

I could've sworn at some point she said, 'Five cats answer my door through the disaster.' I was scratching my head confused. 'What cats? Disaster? Mom . . . Mom?' There was silence for a while, and then I heard a more masculine voice.

'Son?' the voice said.

I smacked myself on the head after I heard his voice because now I understood that my mother wasn't saying anything about cats; she was trying to say, 'I can't do this anymore. Here's your father.'

'Dad!' I said, 'I don't know if you can make any sense of what Mom is going on about but . . .'

My dad chuckled. 'You got the job and the girl. All in a day's work for us Turner men. Good work, kid,' he said.

'What's even more impressive is that you got all of that from the weird demon language that Mom was speaking this whole time.' I quipped.

'I've been married to her thirty years. She got that way when I proposed to her. You and Jenna will have languages of your own thirty years from now,' he said.

I hadn't thought that far into the future, but my father was probably right. Jenna and I would go on to know each other's deepest darkest secrets and one and other's fatal flaws. I could deal with anything Jenna threw at me right now, but maybe there would be worse to come in the future. I was uncertain about how I'd cope with them, but I knew for sure that she was worth learning to cope for.

I hung up with my father; in the background, I could still hear my mother wailing. He said something about coming over later on in the week to talk about some things face to face before he hung up. I didn't think too much of it because my father liked to see me from time to time. If there was a hockey game on TV and the Leafs were playing, then he'd come over and watch it. If the Raptors were playing, I'd go over to his house and force him to watch it with me. He wouldn't drive twenty minutes to my house for a Raptors game because he thought that the basketball team wasn't worth his time. It gave me an excuse to be around him though, so I made sure that was a tradition I kept alive. My mother would always tag along with him when he did drive over. Jenna and she would keep each other entertained somehow or the other. They'd trade recipes and beauty secrets and serve us drinks and snacks while they gossiped about how lazy men were as a species. Most of the times, they would just go out shopping. My dad and I loved it when that happened because it gave us some time alone to talk about work and sports without feeling the need to explain terms like travelling and over-the-back every now and then to the ladies.

I went back into the bedroom, tiptoeing slightly just in case Jenna was still asleep. When I walked in, she was sitting up with her back against the backrest, the blanket still on her up to her waist.

'Good morning,' I said; apparently I had been too loud because shortly after the words escaped my lips, Jenna shushed me and said, 'Not so loud. I'm barely even awake yet.'

I crawled back into the bed next to her and rested my head on her stomach. She ruffled my hair a little and leaned down to kiss the side of my head.

'I had the strangest dream about you cooking me breakfast this morning,' she said to me, still ruffling my hair.

I wanted to sit up straight and give her the foulest look I could muster, but the tone of her voice made it clear to me that she was simply playing around.

'Were the eggs to your liking in this dream?' I asked.

'Who said anything about eggs?' she said with a smile. Even though I couldn't see her face, I knew that she was smiling because every time she spoke with a smile the happiness in her voice was palpable. That was one of the many things I loved about her.

'You don't have to be at work until tomorrow morning, right?' she asked.

I nodded causing her satin nightdress to move with my head.

'Do you want to . . .' I didn't even wait for her to finish that sentence. I got up from off her stomach and kissed her.

'What are you doing? I meant do the laundry!' she said, smiling ever so slyly.

'Oh, that's what I was going to do. Starting with this outfit of yours,' I said as I undid her top.

# FOUR

## POST-IT PROMISES

My alarm didn't go off the following morning. I woke up afraid that I'd be late for my first day. I had managed to mess up my first few minutes with the man who was going to interview me for the job in the first place. I'd hate to imagine the impression my future colleagues would have of me if I showed up late on my first day. Luckily though I managed to wake up a whole forty minutes before I had to get there, which gave me enough time to shower, get dressed, and make the commute over to Downtown Toronto.

Without thinking about the rest of the day, I sprinted to the bathroom and showered. Normally, I'd take as long as I needed in there to get squeaky-clean, but today, I wasn't scoring myself on cleanliness. Instead I was aiming at getting points for speed. That may have been one of the quickest showers of my life, which was the good news. The bad news was that because of running around with water dripping from every inch of my body while scrambling for soaps, towels, and clothes, I managed to make a pretty brutal mess of the bathroom. Jenna hated it when I made a mess. I was generally a messy guy as a bachelor. I never kept my clothes in order, my closet was always a complete disaster, and I had music CDs and other paraphernalia sprawled all over my apartment. All that changed in a hurry when I started living with Jenna. She had done to me what every mother dreamed of doing to her son. She domesticated me. It didn't seem that big of a compromise and eventually I came to appreciate the order in which my things were always kept. Everything had its place in the house and nothing looked cluttered, and for the first time in my life, I knew where to look to find specific things.

I didn't have time to think about the different kinds of hurt Jenna would want to make me feel when she found out that *Hurricane Ollie* had hit her precious bathroom, so I got out of there quickly and tiptoed out of my bedroom so that I didn't wake Jenna up. I must confess: the not-waking-her-up part was not purely because I wanted her to get a good night's rest. I had been afraid that when she'd realise the mess I'd made, Jenna might smother me with a pillow while I sleep. Or worse, revoke my sex privileges!

When I did get to the kitchen, I contemplated cooking breakfast, but then I looked over at the sink and in it sat the pots and pans I had used to cook breakfast for Jenna yesterday . . . Unwashed. *Oops!* Surely there was no way I could clean up the house before I left and still make it in time for work. So I did what anyone would do in that situation. I left it the way it was and hoped to the heavens that my loving and adoring fiancé would forgive me. I grabbed a post-it from the coffee table in the living room and wrote: 'Sorry, babe! I'll clean up when I'm back! Love you xx' on it and stuck it on the refrigerator. I drew a smiley face under it for some reason. I didn't really think it through when I did it, but it seemed like a logical addition at the time.

I scrambled out of the house and made my way to work. Driving there would be pointless because the UTT was situated downtown, and everyone who has lived in Toronto knows that taking a car downtown from the suburbs in rush hour traffic was torture. Even if you did manage that, finding a parking spot would require a miracle. I would have used public transport, but I was running late, and I was uncertain of the quickest route. I'd travelled downtown a million and a half times before, but even I couldn't tell you what mode of transport would get you there in a hurry. Luckily, I didn't have to ponder over this for too long because there was a taxi close by. That almost never happened in the suburb where I lived. You had to be extremely lucky to get a taxi out of the blue in a time like this in Pickering. I ran over to the cab and told the driver to take me to the UTT. It was as popular a landmark as the CN Tower, so he didn't ask me twice.

I got there with less than three minutes to spare. I handed the taxi driver the fare and thanked him before he drove off. I thought about how expensive taking a cab to work every day would be, and it seemed silly to even contemplate because if I did that I'd be spending more money on travelling to and fro from work than I'd be making. *Yep, definitely doing public transport tomorrow onwards.*

I stared up at the UTT in all its glory from the sidewalk below. Every time I saw the structure, it appeared to be more and more fascinating. The fresh morning sunlight bouncing off the glass, the sheer height of the building, and the way it made everything else in the world seem miniscule was awe inspiring. I walked into the revolving door and was greeted by a teenage boy wearing a maroon uniform with horizontal black stripes. He had a matching hat and a gold nametag that read *Oliver Jones*. I noticed that he had a translucent earpiece inside his ear with a coiling wire going down from his collar into his shirt, like the sort of talkback devices that news reporters wear on the field. I could've sworn he wasn't there to greet me the last time I came in.

'You're a new face, sir, where to?' he asked in a happy-to-help sort of way.

'Err . . . it's my first day,' I stammered. I was confused about what to say to him.

'Oh right! You're the newbie. *Trick of the Trade,* right?' he asked, 'Oliver Turner?'

'Yeah, how did you?' his response was speedy, and he didn't need me to elaborate on that question which made me certain that he had been asked this by every person that was ever starting out in the building.

'Oh, I'm just here to make sure that no one who doesn't belong in the building does get through,' he said uncomfortably. I was sure that I had asked too many questions and overstayed my welcome, but I was fascinated by this security system. I wanted to know more, but I figured now was not the time to discuss it with him, so I walked towards the elevators giving him a friendly nod. There were eight elevators spread out the massive lobby. I stared at them, panning from left to right trying to choose one of them.

'Pick any one, sir,' the boy said to me. 'Once you hit the button of your desired floor, it will go non-stop to it. Part of the whole *Intelligent by design* theme we have going on here.'

I was quite impressed by the technology that the building had. I mean, I knew that the building itself took years to build but now I knew why.

The little things that made life simple were part of what made this building a landmark.

'Oh yeah, almost forgot! The elevator won't go past the sixty-seventh floor, so you'll have to stop off there and go up a couple of flights of stairs to get to the top.' he said me matter-of-factly. 'Maintenance issues,' he grumbled.

I pressed the up button on the elevator nearest to the ground floor and waited a few seconds for it to go 'ding!' It opened up, and I got in and hit sixty-seven. I looked down at my watch and noticed that I was now a few minutes late on my first day. *You just had to make small talk with the teenage super security guy!* The elevator moved pretty rapidly considering it had a lot of ground to cover. Within seconds, I was at the sixty-seventh floor. I would've stuck around and marvelled at the offices on that floor, but I had to make time, since I was already late, and I had no idea where the staircases were. I looked around and saw a sign hanging from the ceiling. It didn't have any words on it, but it was made of glass and had green stickers on it of a man running up a flight of stairs. It was simple enough to explain to me that that's where the staircase was. I headed in that direction and sure enough there was a large white door with some stickers on it. I pushed down on the handle that kept it shut and swung it open. The good news: I found the staircase. The bad news: the alarm system had been triggered. I took a step back from the door and read the stickers on it. It read in big bold letters: ***FIRE ESCAPE—DO NOT OPEN UNLESS EMERGENCY SITUATION PRESENTS ITSELF.***

I tried shutting the doors, but they wouldn't close all the way. It was as though the magnetic locks that kept the door shut were electronically controlled to open on all floors if even one of the doors were opened. I would marvel at the advancements of human technology, but the entire sixty-seventh floor was filed in a line behind me. Everyone from the sixty-eighth and sixty-ninth floors fled downstairs from their offices. The elevators had been switched off because it's common sense not to use them in case there was a fire in the building. I had caused a lot of damage already, but I was hoping that no one was trapped in the elevators. I stepped aside from the sea of people that were now standing behind me and tried to explain that there had been a mix-up, but no one was willing to listen. They just ignored me and marched downstairs. I was surprised at how calmly they all were acting as though this was something that happened before. I had only witnessed a fire scare in my high school cafeteria. Everyone knew that someone had just pulled the fire alarm switch to get out of trouble for not doing homework or something but still every kid in the school was sent into frenzy. Even during fire drills, we never managed to stay calm and walk out in a fashionably manner. I learnt quickly that there was no stopping these people from getting downstairs, so I gave in and walked with them. It only took about ten flights of stairs before I heard people talking to each other, saying things like, 'I wonder which moron walked into the wrong staircase this time,' and, 'Oh great! Just what I needed: a walk down a million stairs this early in the morning.'

If you've ever walked down sixty-seven, crowded, flights of stairs before, you'd know what I was going through. The only problem was that I knew that I had myself to blame and everyone else would find out soon enough that there was no fire and some idiot had just opened the wrong door. Sadly, that idiot was me.

When we got downstairs, the fire escape staircase led us out of the building through the rear exit and into the parking lot in the back of the office compound. I had no idea that this place even had a parking lot and yet there it stood the size of a football field. *Sweet! I can bring my car to work starting tomorrow . . . assuming I still have a job after this incident.*

Oliver, the teenage security kid, came out holding two fingers to the ear that I had spotted the earpiece in he was following a much older man in a suit and dark sunglasses. He looked like he was part of a government organization. He had security written all over him. Well, not really but his persona reeked of surveillance and security. He stood there motionless with the boy in his shadow.

'Right,' Oliver said into a microphone that had been stuck onto the inside of his collar. 'Copy that.' He looked up at the back of the giant security guy in front of him. The security man nodded as though the voices in his head had finally spoken and said, 'False alarm! Back to work.' His voice was deep and husky. Everyone grunted and groaned but finally made their way back up to their desks. Thankfully the elevators were back on, so everyone didn't have to walk back up the never-ending staircase.

I don't know whether it was guilt or something else that made me feel like I deserved to be the last one to get back upstairs, but I waited until everyone else got into their offices until there was only Oliver and myself left in the lobby.

'Don't sweat it man,' he said to me. 'Not the first time someone opened that door. They should really consider putting some text on the sign saying . . .' He made gestures with his hands as though he were designing an invisible sign. 'FIRE ESCAPE THIS WAY. NORMAL STAIRCASE THAT WAY'

I smiled a little bit, but I was still worried because it may be an everyday occurrence to everyone in this building, but word must have spread that I was the cause of this impromptu morning exercise drill.

I hailed the elevator and waited for the *ding*, but before it came, Oliver looked at me and said, 'Oh and by the way . . . the staircase you're looking for is just to the left of the elevators. You can't miss it.' He cleared his throat and continued, 'I mean, not twice anyway.'

I made it to the sixty-seventh floor and looked to the left of the elevators. Sure enough, there it was: the staircase. How could I have missed it? *Only you could ruin your first day this badly.* I thought of what I was going to have to deal with when I got into the office, and there were no possible scenarios that came to mind where I did not get fired on my first day.

I walked up to the sixty-ninth floor. My feet were starting to feel sore, but I knew I had no right to complain. I braved it out and walked into the foyer where I sat a couple of days ago.

The secretary at the front desk sat in the same position she had when I first saw her, hacking away at the keyboard in front of her.

'Good morning, Mister Turner,' she said with a toothy smile. 'Mister Astiff asked to see you whenever you walked in.'

'Oh, great,' I said, stifling a cough. *He didn't enjoy the walk downstairs very much,* I imagined.

I began to walk to the big glass door and waited to be buzzed in like I had been when I came here for the interview, but nothing happened. I tried pushing the door, but it did nothing other than create a rattling sound.

'Oh, silly me,' the secretary said. 'Here's your access card.' She held out a small rectangular card no bigger than a credit card. 'This opens every door in the building, logs your in-time and out-time every time you scan it, and a new one will be provided in the event that you lose it, but I would really appreciate if you didn't because the paperwork is just horrific.'

I took the white card and thanked her. I was trying not to seem as excited as I was, but I was sure I was failing to conceal my joy. After all these years of dreaming and hoping, I finally had an all access pass to the UTT, literally! I swiped the card across the scanner, and the door beeped and opened for me. I couldn't help but smile when that happened.

That smile, however, quickly faded because I realised that Mister Astiff wanted to see me and I might never get the chance to use that card ever again.

I summoned the courage to walk into his office. I knocked before entering.

'Come in,' he mouthed.

I walked in and he exclaimed, 'Good to see you finally made it!' I thought he was being sarcastic because thanks to the whole fire scare and everything, I was a whole two hours late for my first day.

'Yeah, I uh . . .' I didn't know how to start explaining what had happened but he cut me off.

'Sorry about the fire alarm thing. I hope that doesn't deter you from staying on with us?' he said.

I realised that my hand had subconsciously made its way to the top of my head and started scratching, making me look like a confused gorilla.

'These things happen far too often for my liking, and frankly, something needs to change,' he said.

I thought about what the security kid said to me downstairs earlier and paraphrased, 'Maybe they should put up a sign on every floor saying, *FIRE ESCAPE THIS WAY. NORMAL STAIRCASE THAT WAY.*'

'Excellent idea, Oliver!' he said while snapping his fingers. I thought he was only humouring me until he picked up his phone and hit the speaker button.

'Becky?' he said into it.

'Yes, Mister Astiff?' The front desk secretary's voice came out of the speaker.

'Arrange a meeting with Mister Jacoby's design team. I'd like to speak with them before this day is over.'

'Right away, Mister Astiff,' Becky said.

Mister Astiff put the receiver down and looked back at me with a smile on his face. 'I knew I didn't make a mistake when I hired you,' he said. 'It's that kind of creativity that I was looking for all along!' He swivelled in his chair behind his desk and looked out into the Toronto skyline from his window. He had a proud look on his face.

'Welcome aboard, son!' he said, turning back in his chair with his arm extended. Needless to say this wasn't the conversation I was expecting when I got to the office. But I took his hand in mine and shook it.

'There's a big sales pitch tomorrow. Probably the biggest one of the year. I'll tell you about it on the way there. Just come and observe how we do things here. Then you can take over from there,' he said.

I nodded eagerly awaiting further instructions. 'Your cubicle is the one in front of my office.' He pointed through the glass door, and I saw it: a nice cosy nook by the corner, far away from the commotion in the rest of the office. *Couldn't have asked for better.*

'You can park your things there and come back tomorrow. That walk downstairs tired the crap out of everyone, so we're all heading home early today,' he said.

I nodded and left his office. I would've apologised, but he didn't seem to blame me for it and I didn't have the guts to tell him otherwise.

I walked over to my cubicle and studied it. It had three walls covered in light brown plywood, a computer on the desk, and a bulletin board behind it. To my left was a wall that sprawled up to a third of the length of the ceiling, partially shutting me off from the rest of the office. I had a swivel chair just like the one in Mister Astiff's office and a metal nameplate on the outside of my cubical that read—*Oliver Turner: Campaign Strategist.*

This habit was getting old, but I had to keep doing it to assure myself that I wasn't in a state of trance –

*My name is Oliver Turner. I'm twenty-six years old, and I have my own desk!*

# FIVE

## CHOKE

I left for home from work early that day, as suggested by my boss Mister Astiff. I was in no particular hurry to get home because I remembered that I left the house in a complete mess and Jenna would kill me. So, I waited for the bus at the bus stop a couple of blocks down from the UTT, and a few minutes later, I got on the bus. The whole bus ride back I thought about my big day tomorrow and what role I would play in what was apparently *the biggest pitch of the year* for the firm. I couldn't wait to tell Jenna about my day and how I caused an evacuation and got away with it. Before I did any of that, I'd have to keep the promise I made on the post-it and clean up the house.

I got off at the stop nearest to my house and decided to walk the rest of the way home because it was only a couple of blocks down and also it was the fall, so the weather was perfect for a mid-afternoon stroll. The maple leaves had just begun to fall covering the sides of the roads and bits of green around the sidewalks with brown and yellow leaves. I loved being in Toronto this time of year. I made a promise to myself years ago that I would never leave Canada in between summer and winter because the weather was just right.

I eventually reached my doorstep and opened the door. Jenna wasn't in the living room, so I thought I'd surprise her by getting the dishes done. I looked into the sink and found that the pots and pans had been cleaned and put back in their usual place in a cabinet above the stove. *Okay so she got busy without me. I hope she's not mad.* I walked into the bedroom assuming I'd find her there, but I realised I was wrong the second I walked into the room.

The bed was still a mess, and it was unlike Jenna to leave things that way. I looked towards the bathroom and noticed that the door was half-opened. I walked towards it and looked inside. The water had dried up, but on the floor, my outfit from the previous night was left unmoved. I left the room and walked out into the kitchen and peeled off my post-it note from the refrigerator. It was still there, the way I had left it. Just as I stuck it back on, I heard voices coming from the backyard. I opened the door that led from the kitchen to the deck that we had in our yard and found Jenna sitting there talking to my mother and father.

'Ollie!' my mom said as she got up off her seat. 'I haven't seen you in weeks!' She came close to me and hugged me with what seemed like every ounce of strength in her frail body.

Whenever my mother hugged me, I felt the sudden urge to go to eat bread. I always thought that was because she had spent most of her life in the kitchen taking care of either my father or myself. All my fondest memories of my mother had the kitchen somewhere in the backdrop. The first time she made cookies when I was a baby, the times I'd get an *A* in school and she'd leave her pots and pans to come over and congratulate me, and she was even in the kitchen the first time she met Jenna. I remembered that day as though it was just yesterday, even though it had been a few years ago. Jenna was so nervous about meeting my parents, even after I had told her how nice and welcoming they both were. It didn't take her a lot of convincing, but eventually she gave in and came with me. My father greeted Jenna at the front door with a warm hug and gave her the tour of the house before she even got a chance to meet my mother. I had already made myself comfortable on one of the kitchen countertops, the way I always did when I was growing up, by the stove where my mother would always be cooking up a storm. I was having a conversation with her when she suddenly stopped what she was doing and walked over to the living room. I didn't know what was happening at the time, but it felt a bit odd. My mother wasn't the sort of person that would ever leave her kitchen that abruptly. While she was walking out of the kitchen, she took off her apron which said '*#1 MOM*' on it and hugged Jenna without saying a word. Jenna was taken aback, but she managed to smile and hug back.

'Ollie told me you were beautiful, but my, was he underplaying it!' I recalled her saying, holding Jenna's hand in hers. Jenna was about half a foot taller than my mother and that was even with my mom's thin blonde hair, sticking out of the bun she tied it in, in all directions.

I snapped out of my flashback and noticed my mother wasn't hugging me anymore. Instead she was running her hand up and down my back and muttering something about how I needed to gain some weight. No sooner did she start doing that than she walked out of the deck and into the kitchen. I wanted to stop her and tell her to sit with me, but I knew how hopeless that was.

As though reading my mind, my father chimed in, 'You know Martha. She doesn't feel like she's at home unless she's in the kitchen.' Jenna smiled at my dad.

My dad stood up and made his way to me, his thin silver-grey hair shining in the sunlight. While he made his way over, I noticed a few things that seemed a bit off. He was wearing a shirt and jeans, which was normal if you didn't know my dad. I, however, knew my dad . . . Him wearing a shirt was anything but normal. He only wore loose T-shirts, and in his mind, dressing up was putting on Polo. The only times he confessed to wearing a shirt were under his tuxedo on his wedding day and the day I graduated. The other thing that made me curious was that he was walking with a slight limp, not as though he had broken his leg but as though he had grown tired of using the muscles in his calves, like he had been walking a lot. He put his arm around my shoulder and looked over at Jenna who was still smiling.

'Son . . .' he said to me, not breaking his gaze on Jenna, 'your mother and I worked very hard to raise you well, and I'm a bit upset.' Jenna's smile began to fade because she was unsure where he was going with this. That made two of us.

'I'm upset that Jenna here is doing a better job of keeping you in-check than we ever could!' he added. My father began laughing when he had finished speaking and Jenna and I joined in. My father stopped to cough and grabbed my shoulder.

'You okay, Dad?' I asked, holding on to him because it seemed as though he was about to tip over.

'Yeah, it's nothing . . .' he said. He probably would've said more, but my mother began yelling from the kitchen.

31

'John!' she screamed. 'I need your help in here, and I can't find anything in this kitchen!'

'Duty calls,' he said, as he patted my back and went into the kitchen, shutting the glass door behind him.

I sat down on the seat next to Jenna, and her head quickly found its way to my shoulder. I immediately kissed her forehead.

'Don't think a kiss is going to make me forget the promise you made me,' she said. I knew she was smiling because her voice did that weird thing that it did whenever she smiled.

I smirked, 'What promise? I have no idea what you're talking about.'

'You're lucky your parents have a spare key. Mom told me about the dishes she had to do and that was even before I woke up,' she said as she lifted her head off my chest and faced me.

'I'll clean up the room,' I said. 'I promised on a post-it, remember? Those things are legally binding!'

'You better because I sure as hell won't.' She was mad but she couldn't help but smile.

She stopped in her tracks as though she had just remembered something. She smacked my thigh with her palm and said, 'Oh my goodness! I almost forgot to ask! How was work?'

I told her about my day and how eventful it had been. She seemed to be certain that only I could have pulled the fire alarm on my first day at work. She did seem impressed that I was been given so much responsibility so early on. The way Mister Astiff had spoken about this deal that he was taking me to oversee the next day had made it seem as though it was one of those high-up-in-the-ranks-only meeting. She didn't share my enthusiasm about having my own desk though. That's probably because she didn't think it was as big a deal as I did. After all, having a desk at the UTT was one of my biggest dreams ever.

'Ollie!' I heard my mom yelling from inside the kitchen. 'Where do you keep the onions?'

'No need to get them. Yeesh! Give me a minute, and I'll find it.' I could hear my father say.

'Nonsense! You couldn't find your shirt this morning and it's been in your closet in the same place for twenty years!' my mom bickered.

I looked over at Jenna, and she rose to her feet giggling.

'Promise you'll help me find onions when we're their age,' she asked as she held out her hand to me.

'Quick . . .' I said, 'Get me a post-it,' as I took her hand and got out of the backyard and walked into the kitchen.

———◆———

After my mom found out where the onions were, she managed to cook up a feast. We all sat at the dining table in the centre of the living room and ate together as one happy, albeit slightly dysfunctional, family.

Our dining table had four chairs and wasn't round like the traditional dining tables. It was a square-shaped one made out of black wrought iron and an off-white slab of marble on the tabletop. On the marble sat a dish containing a lasagne that was so fresh that the cheese on it was still bubbling, a bowl filled with neatly placed loaves of garlic bread, and another bowl filled with stir fried vegetables.

At the dinner table, my father and I talked about a whole bunch of sports that we felt we needed to catch each other up on. Jenna would chime in every now and then, but I was getting the feeling that her knowledge of sports was wearing thin. My mother just kept piling everyone's plates up with more food. There was always more food in my plate than anyone else's. I'd look over at her trying to suggest that if I ate anymore, I'd explode. She'd just smile and say, 'You need to eat more, Ollie. Look at how skinny you've become!'

I kept quiet and kept eating because every time I looked over at my father for sympathy, he'd just shrug and stare at the mountain of food that seemed to be in his plate as well. He kept eating, and the food didn't seem to disappear. He was eating awfully quickly too. I asked him to slow down a couple of times, but he didn't think that he was doing anything out of the ordinary. Eventually though I proved to have been right because he went into a coughing fit like I've never seen before. He was clutching his chest with both his hands and coughing as he pushed his chair away from the table.

'He's choking!' I yelled as I sprang up and grabbed him trying to perform the Heimlich manoeuvre.

'Ollie, no!' my mother yelled as she reached out to me.

I was persistent though, as was my father's cough.

'If I stop, he could die, Mom!' I yelled back still lifting my dad a few inches off the ground as I squeezed. His coughing was slowly turning into a wheeze.

Eventually, he stopped coughing and I put him down. He was panting and holding onto his chest, kneeling over the table.

'Dad!' I said with tears in my eyes.

'Son . . .' he said as he looked up at me, still breathing heavily.

'You weren't choking, were you?' I asked, taking a step back from him.

'No, son,' he said, finally sitting back down on his chair.

'We knew a few months ago but didn't know how to . . .' my mother said, breaking into tears.

'Tell me what?' I said, looking over to my dad for answers.

'Son,' he said, looking into my eyes, 'I have cancer.'

# SIX

## FIRE DRILL

After dinner, my mom and Jenna cleaned up in the kitchen. My father and I sat in the living room watching a rerun of an old basketball game. No one said a word; we just sat there in silence. I hugged my parents goodbye shortly after, and they left. Jenna and I made our way to the bedroom but neither of us slept. I was sad and furious at the same time. The only thing I was thinking was that there were so many worse people in the world that deserved cancer. I'd never wish it on anyone, but even still I couldn't shut the thoughts from my mind. My father was the nicest man I'd ever known. He kept to himself as much as he could and never ruffled any feathers. He didn't smoke, and he didn't have any bad habits. He had the occasional beer with me, but he was far from being an alcoholic. If I had to write down a list of people that should've gotten cancer instead, the list would be endless, but if I had to write one on the people that should never have gotten it, my father would be the only one I could think of.

Jenna held my head in her arms. I would've cried, but I was too furious to give up. She knew better than to tell me anything because at this point, I wouldn't know what to believe. Instead she just played with my hair and kept awake with me until the sun came up. Eventually she fell asleep with me still on her chest. As for me, sleep was definitely not on the cards.

I got out of bed and pulled the blanket over Jenna and moved her pillow to support her neck in a less awkward manner. I quickly got ready and left for work early that day.

I didn't know how long the drive was, and I honestly wasn't paying much attention to the drive there. Under other circumstances, I'm sure

35

I'd appreciate the emptiness of the roads this early in the day, but today wasn't one of those days. When I reached the UTT building, I noticed there were three cars in the parking lot before me. I thought about it for a second and concluded that there was no way anyone drove to work earlier than I did. The fact that their cars were still here meant that they had spent the night at work.

I parked in one of the spots furthest from the entry. I assumed that since I was new here, the older employees probably thought that they had earned bragging rights over the parkings closer to the entry and also I could use the little bit of walking to clear my head.

I walked into the building, and Oliver, the adolescent security chief, was in the lobby going through something on his checklist.

'Good day to you, sir . . .' he said, not looking up from his checklist, 'early start today?'

'Just thought I'd beat traffic,' I said, although I was sure I wasn't entirely convincing.

I began walking away towards the elevators, and I noticed that Oliver had looked up and in my direction. I didn't want to make conversation with him, so I kept walking along. It wasn't that I didn't like the kid or anything; it was just that my dad had just told me that he had cancer. I didn't want to talk to anyone that I didn't need to talk to. The less I said today, the better it would be for everyone.

'Everything has a reason,' he said just before he looked back down at his checklist.

I looked back to where he was standing with a confused expression on my face.

'When you think there's no logical explanation for something,' he said, tapping a pen on his clipboard, 'something or someone shows you the way.'

I stepped back a little, unsure of how he had just gotten into my mind. I felt like a door had been opened into my brain and he had just peered into it. *I just said all that stuff out loud, didn't I?*

I didn't realise until he looked back at me that I was still giving him that confused expression. He smiled at me and said, 'I was talking about you opening the fire escape door. You know that whole signage thing . . . Someone took the advice and they put up signs telling people where to go if they don't want to make Mister Astiff unhappy.'

'I'm sure more people were annoyed about having to walk all the way down than just Mister Astiff,' I said.

'Well, no one hates being made to move around more than absolutely necessary than Mister Astiff. Why do you think the entire office was sent home early?' he replied.

'Nonsense,' I said. 'I'm sure Mister Astiff is just as active as anyone else his age. He must've had other reasons to stop work.'

Oliver just smiled at me and looked back down at his clipboard. 'You'll see,' he said. 'Still gotta get off on the sixty-seventh floor though. Maintenance isn't done yet.'

I nodded and hit floor number sixty-seven on the elevator panel. It wasn't long until I had reached my destination, but the silence in the elevator felt good. It was a shame I had to be in this foul a mood on my first real day at work. I would've taken a personal day, but after my antics on my first day here, I didn't want to seem like a brat. Since I had to be at the office, I might as well as make the best of it. Before I walked out of the elevator, I promised myself that I would shut out my personal life from my professional one and go about the day as normal. After work I would go straight to my father's house and watch some TV with him. Telling myself that made me feel instantly better. I heaved a sigh and walked towards the staircase. (The right one this time.)

After climbing up the two flights of stairs, I walked into the main waiting area of my office, *The Trick of the Trade*, and Becky greeted me good morning.

'Are you always in this early?' I asked, surprised to see her at her desk way before anyone else should've even gotten out of bed.

'I make it a point to always be here at least an hour before everyone else does.' She said, 'Gives me a head start.'

Becky was so much like a robot that sometimes I forgot that she was a real person. The only time she'd look away from her computer screen was to say something to the person she was talking to. When she did look at you, she'd have this wide grin that went from ear to ear, thus revealing her sparkling white teeth that could give the big chandeliers in the office lobby a run for their money. The smile was so forced that it made her whole face look strained. She made it look as though smiling was too much of an effort for her cheeks to bear. The whole time she would be hacking away at her keyboard non-stop. I was so amazed at how much that woman could type that the grin wasn't even what set me off most about her anymore.

I cut my conversation with Becky short. I nodded and approached the door. I was afraid that if I said anything, she'd break her gaze from the computer screen and smile at me. You know how they'd say that, *The eyes are a window to the soul.* Well, in her case, it was, *The teeth are a mirror that will blind your soul.*

I pulled out my key card from my pocket and swiped it on the door, and they magically opened for me. I'd have to admit, no matter how often I'd have to do that it would always amuse me that I had the power to open any door in this building.

'Even the ones you shouldn't,' a deep and manly voice said from somewhere near me. After that had been said, a woman laughed. I thought that someone from the office had figured out that it was me that triggered that false alarm yesterday. When I looked around, I saw a brunette wearing a purple shirt and black skirt who was sitting on a desk that was occupied by a man, who appeared to be in his mid-thirties wearing a shirt and blazer over denim jeans. His brown hair was parted slightly to the side, and he looked like he was the sort of guy who looked as prim-and-proper as he was now even when he had just gotten out of bed.

The woman was still laughing. The man continued speaking, 'It's amazing, right? So I told Brianna that I could have any girl I wanted and I still stayed married to her.' The brunette was still laughing uncontrollably. Maybe it was because I just walked in but that joke wasn't funny at all. *She's probably in love with that guy. Poor thing.* 'You cross all lines, even the one you shouldn't!' he added. So it was clear that they weren't talking about me. The woman looked up and noticed me and stopped laughing. She cleared her throat and sat up of the desk. 'See you later, Brad,' she said, straightening her skirt. The man, who I could only assume was called Brad, looked over in my direction and cleared his throat, 'Erm, yeah see you later, Francine.' He said while turning back to look at Francine walk away.

I began walking away feeling as though I had made both of them uncomfortable, but Brad stood up and walked towards me. 'Hey, new guy!' he said as he approached. 'Oliver, right?'

'Yeah, and you're Brad?' I said, shaking his hand.

'So you heard that, eh?' he asked.

'I didn't mean to . . . I . . . I . . .' I honestly had no idea how to finish that sentence. What would I have said? *Yes. I was eavesdropping.* Or *nah, you just looked like someone that'd be called Brad.*

Luckily he cut me off, 'Don't sweat it man. Francine is like a sister to me.'

*Sister? Yeah right.*

'Anyway, Rob asked me to get you up to speed on the pitch whenever you walked in.'

'Rob? The pitch?' I asked, confused.

'Jesus, bro! Robert Astiff, Rob? You know, your boss? And how are you not familiar with the whole once in a lifetime deal? Biggest our firm has ever had? Am I ringin' any bells here, bro?' he asked, punching the air with each derogatory question he threw at me.

'Oh, right!' I cleared my throat. 'Sorry, I'm a bit flustered today.'

'It's cool. It's cool,' he said, now sparring with the air. 'Anyway, let's meet at your desk in a second. I have to go to the little boy's room first.' He smacked my shoulder and walked away.

It was way too early in the day for anyone to be that hyper. Someone must've laced his coffee with some Red Bull, or he must've consumed so much candy as a kid that the sugar high never wore off.

I rubbed my shoulder with one hand, because I could feel the smack starting to sting a little, and walked towards my desk.

I sat down at my desk and noticed I had left my computer on from yesterday. The screen saver was on. It was a slideshow of different pictures of the *UTT*. Each picture reminded me why I loved this building so much and how great an honour it was to have a desk in an office in the building. When I looked back up from my computer screen, I noticed that people had already made their way to their desks and cabins. A few minutes ago, the office was empty barring the presence of only Francine, Brad, and *the walking talking billboard for Crest 3D White*: Becky the secretary.

Brad was making his way back from the restroom on the far end of the office, right by where the water cooler was. He stopped for a millisecond at each person's desk and pointed his fingers as though he were holding a gun. He made a strange clicking sound and winked at people he passed by. *Why does he insist on being such a douche?*

After what seemed like twenty 'Hello's' (at gunpoint, or dare I say finger point), he finally got to my desk.

'So there's this big Soda firm that wants to get strategies from us on their new campaign,' he said.

'What Soda firm?' I asked.

'I can't tell you the name because they haven't told us yet. They plan on keeping it a secret until they finish the campaign.'

'So they won't even tell us?' I asked, confused.

'Us? They won't even tell their own employees the damn name,' he was the sort of guy that cut to the chase when he spoke. I liked that about him because today out of all days I needed that. *If you must talk to me today, let it be about work . . . Say it quickly and go away.*

'So how are we going to build a campaign around something so secretive?' I asked, scratching my head.

'They're paying us three million dollars to figure that out for them,' he said, tapping his fingers on my desk to the tune of what was obviously some *Death Metal* song, because it annoyed the daylights out of me.

I sat back in my chair and swivelled a little, unintentionally. What kind of Soda Company had three million to spare before even coming up with a name? *3,000,000 Dollars; that's a three with a whole bunch of zeroes after it.*

'So today's meeting is where Rob and I go in there and try to get some details from these suckers as to what they're looking at for their brand,' he said as he stretched his arms. *Oh good! He's getting tired.* He jumped up off his makeshift seat on my table and started jogging back to his desk. 'Oh and with any luck, we'll stifle some more money out of those fuckers!' he said, his voice fading as he got further and further away from my desk.

'Mind your language!' some lady screamed from the crowd. Brad continued jogging and waved his hand in the air and said, 'Sorry, my bad!'

*I guess I was wrong; he doesn't tire easily after all.*

I think Brad was on his third lap of the office when Mister Astiff walked into the office looking grumpy. Brad stopped at the door and walked with Mister Astiff towards his cabin in front of my desk. I couldn't tell what Brad was saying, but he was talking fast and Mister Astiff looked as though he was about to crumple the newspaper in his hand and smack Brad upside the head with it. Instead he kept walking and nodding to what Brad was saying. When they got close to the cabin, Brad turned around and went to his desk. Mister Astiff came to my desk before he went into his cabin.

'Oliver!' he said, 'Brad told me he got you up to speed on the whole secret Soda deal. The meeting is just after lunch so that gives Brad and myself a few hours to go through the details.' I didn't like the way he said *Brad and myself*. I thought I was part of this dream team. 'Do you need my help with anything, sir?' I asked hoping he'd fill me in.

'No, that won't be necessary. Your expertise is required for the later stages of this campaign. Today, I just want to introduce you to the people we're dealing with . . . Let them know you exist.' He walked away before he finished his last sentence and entered his cabin without looking back at me.

I felt like I had psyched myself up too much for just an introduction. I was ready to be prepped and take this campaign head on. I would dwell on the fact that today was going to be a let-down, but there were more pressing concerns. The fire alarm had gone off again, and Brad was making a wailing noise, trying to impersonate a fire truck, yelling, 'Fire! Fire! Fire! Fire!' He went on to mimic the sound of the alarm. Everyone in the office looked furious as they filed into one line and walked out of the office. Francine stood next to Brad who kept doing his annoying impersonation, of what I could only imagine was a fire truck with Down syndrome and laughed. I was last in the line, partly sad because I had to walk down sixty-nine flights of stairs and partly happy because I wasn't the one that caused it this time.

I looked into Mister Astiff's cabin, and he sat there reading his newspaper, completely ignoring the madness ensuing outside.

I knocked on his door and walked in. 'Sir, the alarm has gone off. Aren't you coming?'

'Oh, I won't be joining you guys in this madness. I've already been made to walk up two flights of stairs. I refuse to walk another step,' he said, sternly.

'But, sir, what if there's actually a fire?' I was genuinely concerned because the chances of that happening were quite high considering the fact that I was in the office and far away from fire-escape door opening range. This could very well be a real fire.

'If there is a fire, I'll burn to the ground with this building.' He didn't look up from his paper. 'Beats having to walk down sixty-nine flights of stairs.'

I gave up, reluctantly, and walked out into the fire escape staircase with everyone else. Everyone had left when the alarm kicked in. The only two people that stayed behind were Brad and Becky. Unfortunately, since I was the last to walk out of the office, I had the *pleasure* of walking down with the two of them. *I'm sure that my dad, with his cancer and everything, will be having more fun than I will for the next twenty or so minutes.*

This was the first time in my life that I had seen Becky stand up. I was staring at her as though I was shocked to have discovered that she did, in fact, have a lower body. Brad held out his hand hoping she'd take it. 'Hold on to me for protection,' he said to her, ignoring the fact that I was standing right next to him.

Becky smiled, and even though I wasn't looking directly at her, I could see the shine from her overly white teeth bounce off the walls. 'I'd rather be set ablaze by this fire.'

Brad didn't give up though. *He's resilient; I'll give him that.* He kept on hitting on her flight after flight after flight of never-ending staircase. The sad part was that Becky was beginning to give in to Brad's childish charms. She began opening up and encouraging him by looking at him with wistful eyes. I think it was on the forty-something-th floor when she hit him on his shoulder gently and blushed. He had said something to the effect of, 'It's good to see more than just your top half . . . Not that it's bad, I could stare at it all day, but those legs! Oof! Those bad boys shouldn't be kept a secret from the world!'

There were about four, maybe five more moments where I wanted to barf, but I stayed strong and just kept walking. I would've tried breaking away from the two of them, but Brad kept racing down a flight of stairs mid-sentence, stopping at the bottom for us to catch up. I was afraid of speeding up because if I had overtaken him at any point, he would think I wanted to race with him down the stairs. If that did happen and he bolted down the stairs, I'd be left with no one but Becky for company and I didn't want it to be awkward all the way down.

After what seemed like three years, we reached the bottom. My feet were as sore as a herd of goats' hooves after climbing up a mountain. I should've felt this way yesterday, but the guilt was probably overrunning the pain at that point.

The big muscular man in the black suit whom I had seen the day before stood in front of the assembly of people standing in front of him with a finger in his ear, waiting for the voices in his head to tell him something.

Oliver, the adolescent security guard, was nowhere to be seen this time around.

'There was a small technical error on the sixty-eighth floor's elevator shaft,' the big man said in the squeakiest voice I had ever heard. I looked over at everyone amazed at how they all kept a straight face. I wanted to roll on the ground and laugh. It was as though the Giant from Jack and The Bean Stalk spoke in Thumbelina's voice. He cleared his throat with a huge crackle and his normal deep voice returned, 'A few sparks were released from one of the elevator cables, and we had to drive you people out just in the rare event that those sparks caused a fire. We have scanned the premises and there is no more threat. You may resume work.'

People began walking towards the lobby and then the man spoke again, 'Elevator number 1, that is the first one to the left of the lobby, is shut down for further inspection. Please refrain from queuing up there.'

There was something about that man that commanded attention. When he spoke, the whole crowd stood still and began to move only when he stopped speaking. No one would like to admit it, but they were all afraid of him.

I wasn't kind enough to wait for everyone to leave this time around. I wanted to get back to my desk and sit down for a few minutes. I hadn't slept a wink the night before and fatigue was just beginning to kick in. To top it all, I had that big meeting later on in the day. *Could my day get any worse?*

When I walked out of the elevator, my cell phone began vibrating in my pocket. The name on the screen flashed. Jenna was calling. For a brief moment, I felt as though the universe knew I needed to hear her voice. It was like miraculously she knew that I was upset and the only thing that would cheer me up was her smiley voice.

Unfortunately, there was no smile on her voice, for the news that she had to tell me could not be shared with a smile.

She told me that my father had been moved into the Emergency Room, his cancer was getting worse.

# SEVEN

## RING

My original impulse was to double back, get into the elevator I had just gotten out of, and go straight to the hospital to check on my father; however, I didn't get that chance because since I didn't wait downstairs, the elevators' buttons were being pushed frantically. If I did take the elevators back down, I'd be stopped on every floor along the way by people that wanted to get to the floors they desired. I'd have to take the stairs back down. Again.

Before I did that, I thought of getting into the office where I knew my boss would be. Robert Astiff never paid any attention to the fire alarm; he knew the building was safe, for the most part, so I hoped he would be seated at his desk.

Luckily, he was. I wasted no time explaining to him that I needed to leave as soon as I possibly could. He stood up from his chair, patted me on my back, and sent me off on my way.

'Let me know if there's anything you need from me, son!' he said, reassuringly.

I nodded and sprinted back towards the staircase from where I began my descent, for the second time that day.

There was a whirlwind of thoughts rummaging through the insides of my skull. I didn't know what to calculate first: how long the commute would take me, would my father be alive when I got there, or whether or not Jenna was doing a good job of keeping my mother calm. As the thoughts went fluttering by, so did the numbers on the side of walls,

46

indicating which floor I was currently on. I started out on floor 68, what felt like only, a few moments ago. Apparently I was wrong, there was no way I could've reached floor 23 this quickly. I was making good time, and I didn't think it was a bad thing because I needed to be quick. A few moments later, I noticed the number on the wall said 2, which meant I had two floors to go, and only two floors to shut my mind up. I was panting, and I could feel my calf muscles yearning for a break, which wasn't soon to come. I tried gathering my breath while running down, and suddenly, I felt as though something intangible had suspended my left leg in the air, disallowing it from hitting the ground. I tripped down an entire flight of stairs down to the lobby where there were a few people; among which Oliver, the young boy who greeted me in the morning each day, was the first to run to me and help me get back to my feet.

'Are you okay?' he said while dusting my shirt.

'I'm fine, really. Thanks.'

People were staring at me with their jaws hung low, hands covering their mouths, and eyes wide open. I don't know exactly how that looked to them, but from my point of view, it was quite a tumble. I remember seeing lights, ground, lights, and ground and then finally marble. Even still, I wasn't lying about feeling fine. There was no pain other than a slight tingling sensation along the length of my abdomen on the right side of my body and an annoying ringing sound, similar to the fire alarm, in my right ear.

I brushed it off and paid no heed to anyone in the lobby. I resumed walking to my car. My calf muscles weren't even hurting. *Must be the adrenaline.*

I got to my car and set off to see my dad.

The thoughts didn't stop tumbling through my mind, but somehow I had made it to the hospital in, arguably, one piece. I got to the waiting room and saw my mother and Jenna sitting in chairs outside looking calmer than I had expected.

Jenna jumped out of her seat when she saw me and came to hug me.

'What's going on, is he okay? I got here as soon as I could.'

'He's okay now. They're keeping him here for observation,' Jenna told me.

I walked over to my mother and hugged her. She was smiling, which gave me a sense of hope. My mother was never the sort that would smile in the face of adversary, but there she stood braving the storm.

'Who are you and what have you done with, Mom?' I said, partly joking and partly concerned.

She laughed. 'Son, we've been prepared for a lot worse than this for a while now. It's all part of God's plans.'

It amazed me that she could say that. I had only known about my father's condition for a day now. Surely, I couldn't be as calm and collected as her. She'd understand if I had a mental breakdown, but then I knew what effect that would have on her. If she was going to be a trooper through this ordeal, then I guess that meant that I would have to be too. Jenna smiled at me and held my hand. Surely, she knew what was going on in my head, and she was proud of the decision I had made.

'You should go see him now,' my mom said, patting my thigh. 'He needs his rest though so try not to take too long.'

'Take too long? I'll stay here with him!' I said.

'Don't be silly, Ollie! I've already brought an overnight bag. We'll be fine. I have Jenna on speed dial if I need anything. We'll be out of here sooner than you think.' She said, '13B, that's the room he's in.' She looked towards the far side of the corridor.

She really wasn't kidding about being prepared. I wanted to argue, but the woman would normally be a wreck in this case. I thought it was just a front at first, but she was amazingly calm and believable through the whole thing. I didn't feel the need to argue. She would be better prepared than I would to deal with anything if the time was at hand.

I simply nodded and walked towards the corridor and stopped when I got to 13B. The door was partially opened, so I just walked in.

There are some things that you just cannot un-see: my father standing over a chair folding his trousers wearing a hospital gown that exposed his rear end for the world to see, while he faced his back towards me, was one of those things.

'Holy crap, son!' he said, clutching on to his gown trying to cover himself up. 'No one teach you to knock?'

He had an IV drip pricked into his veins, and he almost got tangled up in it.

He was looking a lot better than I thought he would. It was as though there was nothing wrong with him.

I tried holding back the laughter, but I was unsuccessful. My father's face was turning pink, but he turned around and walked sideways back to his bed, undoing the tangles in the tubes of his drip.

I took a seat on the cot by his bedside.

'I didn't want you to see me like this,' he said, covering himself with a blanket.

'I know! If there was ever a side of you I did not want to see, it would have to be your backside.'

'I meant with the needle in my arm, but I guess that's more frightening than anything else I could've thrown at you.' He laughed and then coughed a little.

'You look fine, Dad,' I said, clutching his shoulder.

'Try telling that to your mother. I said I felt a little bit of pain in my chest, and she called Jenna saying my condition worsened. I told her it was nothing but you know how your mother gets.'

I smiled and tried to hide a tear.

'The doctors say there's nothing wrong too, but they want to keep me here for observation or something like that.' He looked frustrated. 'Can you believe that? Observation? Like I'm an endangered bird in a Zoo.'

If there were ever a time where I thought I could spend all day just talking and laughing with my father, tonight would be one of those times. I couldn't stay for longer though because my mother had made it to the door and informed us that the visiting hours had ended and that she bribed the nurses with promises of home-made cookies for three more minutes. The hospital had a rule about no more than one visitor at a time, so she had to say what she had to quickly and stay by the door when she said it and then leave.

I said goodbye to my father and left the room with a smile on my face. It was clear to me now why my mother was so calm. My father was okay, for the most part.

I went back to the waiting room and sat beside Jenna. She rested her head on my shoulder and clutched my hand in hers.

'Have a good day at work?' she asked.

I winced in pain a little bit as she began to squeeze my palm. She inspected it and found that there was a bruise just under my wrist and above my forearm.

'How did you . . . ?'

'I had a bit of a run in with a flight of stairs,' I said.

She shrugged and gave me a look that could only mean one thing, 'Oh boy!'

'You should see the other guy,' I said.

She smiled and held my hand again, this time softer.

Jenna whispered something in my right ear. I nodded, and we left the hospital, hand-in-hand.

I don't know exactly what she said because the ringing in my ear had started getting louder and more prominent. I only agreed because the only sense I could make of what she said was of the words—hot chocolate and cuddles. *My name is Oliver Turner, and I'm a sucker for cuddles.*

After two days of staying awake, a fall down a flight of stairs, and seeing my dad's rear end, nothing would come close to the feeling of a good night's rest in the arms of the most perfect woman in the world. I was lucky enough to have experienced that feeling firsthand last night. I had woken up fresh for work the next day, and I was ready to finally get to work on that presentation. The ringing in my ear hadn't stopped completely, but it had begun to fade away a little bit. It didn't bother me too much as I focused on getting ready and cleaning up after myself.

I put on a nice formal shirt that was black and had a single breast pocket on the left side; it had a red trim running down the left side of the buttons. I put on brown trousers and wore my hair messy. After doing this, I neatly disposed of what I was wearing the day before and put the outfit in the laundry hamper in our bathroom. I didn't want to make another post-it promise I couldn't keep to Jenna. When I thought about that promise, I realised that it had been a while since I had made one. I reached for the pad and wrote—*Date night tonight? I'll buy you flowers, I promise.*

I stuck it on the refrigerator and left for work feeling hopeful that today would be a great day. Any day would be a great day if compared to yesterday. *I should write that down.*

I got to work with a few minutes to spare. I hadn't spoken to Mister Astiff to let him know if I would be coming in today or not, so I thought I'd get there before him and greet him at the door instead.

When I got into the office, it looked like everyone had been there all night. Even Becky the secretary looked tired. She greeted me at the door as I walked by.

I went straight to Mister Astiff's office and knocked on the door. He was in the room with Brad and Francine. The three of them headed towards me in unison, with Mister Astiff leading the way.

'Everything okay, Oliver?' he asked. 'I didn't think you'd be coming in today.'

'Oh yeah, thanks for everything yesterday,' I said. I explained to them that my father was okay and that he was being kept there under observation. Brad pulled out a chair for me. 'Hey, man, take a seat . . . Now that you're here, we can get some fresh new ideas on this presentation.'

'Oh, great!' said Mister Astiff. 'This again.' He walked back to his seat and sat down. I sat in between Francine and Brad, facing Mister Astiff.

'So the client is a soda company,' Brad said.

'He knows that!' shouted Mister Astiff.

'Just getting him up to speed, sir,' Brad said.

Mister Astiff shut his eyes and rubbed his temple with his hands.

Before Brad could continue, he was interrupted by a knock on the door. Becky had come into the room.

'Yes, Becky, what is it?' Mister Astiff said, looking up.

'Sir, I . . . I tried to stop them, but . . .' Becky walked into the room and was followed by two men in almost identical suits. Just by looking at them, I knew they were expensive. The men were almost the same height. They stood just under six feet tall and both had brown hair. One of the men was darker than the other in terms of complexion, and he was the one that spoke to Mister Astiff.

'Robert . . . Good to see you again,' he said.

Mister Astiff stood up and greeted them. 'Henry, Mitch . . . Good to see you both. Please take a seat!' he said and snapped his fingers while looking over at Becky. Becky sprang out of the room and fetched two chairs as though she had just materialised them.

The chairs were placed oddly around the table in Mister Astiff's office, and it was beginning to feel a little claustrophobic.

Mister Astiff got back to his seat and began introducing everyone.

'Henry and Mitchell are the representatives of the firm that's doing this campaign,' he said, looking over at Brad, Francine, and myself. 'This is Francine. She's from the Creative Department.' She nodded and smiled as she said hello. 'This is Brad. He's our marketing analyst.'

'Pleasure to meet you both,' he said, standing up from his seat and shaking each man's hand individually.

Mister Astiff then turned to me. 'This is Oliver, and he's going to strategise this whole campaign.'

That statement took me aback. I knew that they wanted me in on this campaign, but I didn't know that they were putting me in front of the whole operation. I nodded, as though this was not news to me, shook their hands while smiling. I was certain I looked like an idiot because of how wide my smile was, but I couldn't control that.

'Nice to finally meet you guys,' the lighter skinned man said. 'I'm Henry, and this is Mitchell.'

'You can call me Mitch,' said the slightly darker man.

Mister Astiff cut the pleasantries short. 'So tell me, gentlemen, to what do I owe this pleasure?'

'Well, we have some news,' Henry said.

'Good or bad?' asked Brad.

'Just news,' said Mitch.

'How is that even possible?' said Brad, visibly confused. 'All news is either good or bad.'

He was cut short by Mister Astiff. 'That's enough, Brad.' He said, 'What's the news?'

Mitch cleared his throat and loosened his tie. I hadn't even noticed that he was wearing a tie before. I looked over and noticed that Henry wasn't wearing one. *How did I not notice this?* When I was thinking about that, I realised that there were more pressing concerns than fashion statements. I should have been curious as to what the news was, but anything about this campaign, at this point, would be news to me.

'We need the first pitch tomorrow,' Mitch said.

'Tomorrow?' said Mister Astiff, alarmed. 'That's impossible? We didn't agree on a timeline for this . . .' He wanted to say more, but Henry raised his palm indicating that Mister Astiff should stop talking.

'If you are incapable, feel free to back off at any point. We will find another firm to do the job.'

Brad was staring at both sides of the table as though there were a table tennis game in session. He glanced at the men with his jaws wide open and then at Mister Astiff to hear the response.

'So you guys are here to threaten us?' Mister Astiff said.

'No,' replied Mitch, 'just here to help you guys speed things up.'

I was beginning to sweat a little bit because I was unsure how I was going to strategise for this moment, leave alone this entire campaign. I thought about it for a little while and then the ringing in my right ear began again. It was soft, so I decided to try and ignore it.

'What do you have on the marketing gimmick?' Mitch asked Brad.

'Well, we were thinking of a dozen ideas all night last night and we couldn't find one that would really work,' he said.

'So you have nothing?' said Henry, bluntly.

'Not entirely nothing,' chimed in Francine.

She was sitting so quiet the entire time I forgot that she was even in the room.

'We have a couple of ideas that involve marketing the brand itself as nameless, like blank hoardings all over the city with teasers as to what the ad could be about,' she said, looking over at Mister Astiff for support.

Mister Astiff did take the cue and continued, 'You know, like campaigning for the campaign.'

'That's been done before,' said Henry to Mitch. Mitch nodded and confirmed.

'We came to you for new ideas. This isn't new,' Henry said.

'Like we said, there were a few ideas that were not worth working on and then there were some that were even worse . . . It will take longer than one day,' Brad said.

'What's your strategy?' Mitch said, looking over at me.

I looked over at Mister Astiff, trying to get some help on this one because I didn't want to seem like a fool. Mister Astiff just sat back in his chair and sighed. He knew this meeting was going downhill. I had to sound like I knew what was going on. To make things worse, the ringing in my ear was becoming increasingly annoying and louder by the second.

I scratched my ear for a brief moment and resumed attempting to ignore it. The sound didn't go away, but I had stalled for long enough. I had to come up with something.

'I was thinking that we could serve up the soda in restaurants for free and have people ask what it was. When the waiters would come back, they could say that they didn't know. Then we could market it using word of mouth instead of a real campaign.'

I shut my eyes after I said this, trying to make sense of it all in my head.

'No,' said Henry.

'No?' asked Mister Astiff. I noticed that our team had a smile on their faces. What I said didn't make sense to Henry and Mitch but at least the smile reassured me that it was better than anything Mister Astiff, Brad, and Francine could come up with.

'The product isn't ready yet. We can't serve it if it doesn't exist.'

Brad was getting impatient, the way he'd always get when he was made to sit for too long. He began to interrupt anything that anyone was saying. Henry and Mitch weren't fazed by this and went on dealing with the situation calmly. Their calmness was making Mister Astiff livid because he had no control over the matter, and he hated not being in control. Francine just sat there chewing her nails, and as for me, I was sitting there trying to shut out the mind-numbing ringing in my ear.

When the yelling was almost insufferable, Becky walked in.

'Not now, Becky!' Mister Astiff yelled.

'Mister Jacoby is on line two for you,' she said. 'He said it's urgent.'

The yelling didn't die down at all. Brad kept hurling ideas at Henry and Mitch, and the two of them were just shutting down everything that Brad threw at them. Francine sat there chewing her nails. Mister Astiff kept ignoring everything that Becky was saying and yelling at the two suited men in front of him. Becky kept cutting in reminding Mister Astiff that there was a call for him, but she remained ignored.

All this wasn't even half as painful as the ringing. *Oh that damn ringing!* I couldn't take it anymore. I shut my eyes and covered my face until all that there was, was darkness and that painful ring, a ring so sharp and loud that it made my head rattle. I pressed my fingers into my eyes trying to feel something, anything but that incessant ringing. Finally, the ringing got so loud that it felt as though it couldn't get any louder.

Then it stopped.

There was silence. I moved my hands and opened my eyes. I had to squint because there was a sharp light coming at me from all directions. While my eyes readjusted, I snapped my finger next to my right ear to see if I could hear it. I could; it still worked. When my eyes finally readjusted, I looked around and found that I was standing in the middle of a desert. There was nothing but sand under my feet for miles and miles. I was still wearing my black shirt and trousers. My hair was just the way it was this morning, but my wallet wasn't in my pants back pocket where it usually was. It was warm but breezy. Brad, Francine, Mister Astiff, Becky, Henry, and Mitch were nowhere in sight. Mister Astiff's office couldn't have just magically transformed into this! It was all too real to be a dream and yet there was no explaining it.

One minute, I was in a heated meeting, and the next minute, I found myself in the middle of nowhere with no money and nothing to identify myself with.

*My name is Oliver Turner. What on God's green Earth is happening?*

# EIGHT

## ANGEL

I had been walking for hours. The sun showed no sign of give, and it kept tormenting me. The sand beneath my feet was starting to feel like I was walking on fiery hot lava. I had no idea where I was because all around me was nothingness, massive amounts of sand and nothingness, in all directions. I thought about sitting still for a while, but what good would that do? It wouldn't give me any answers as to what the hell actually happened that brought me here. I kept telling myself that I would wake up from this nightmare and get back into that meeting room with Brad, Becky, Francine, and Mister Astiff. Even the part of my brain that came up with that story refused to believe it. I had no idea where I was and even fewer ideas as to what had gotten me there. I eventually decided to walk towards the horizon. My throat and lips were starting to dry out, and I gave myself another twenty minutes before I died of thirst.

The sun had started to set, and I kept following it until it was at eye level. I knew I needed to pick a direction and head in it. I didn't want to be going around in circles all day in a desert, so west would be as good a direction as any. The pain in my calves from walking up and down the flights of stairs began to resurface, and I began to worry as to whether or not the ringing in my ear would start all over again as well. *That'll be the last thing I need.*

A few feet away from where I was standing, I noticed that the sand was beginning to slope downwards and thin out. That must've meant that the desert was ending nearby. It could mean a lot of things, but that was what I was going to tell myself at that point.

I walked rapidly hoping to see some signs of civilisation but none came. Even the sun had left me. I was officially alone now. Luckily, there was a full moon out, so I did have some form of light to guide me as I trudged aimlessly into the ever-open arms of death. The sand that was so hot beneath my feet mere hours ago was now cooling off, releasing what felt like an invisible layer of steam upwards onto my body with every step that I took forward. My throat was drier than it had ever been before. I could feel the cracks upon my lips, but I stopped trying to lick them every now and then. I realised that saliva was all I had to keep me from coughing up a lung. The pain in my feet was too much to bear, all of a sudden. There was so much happening at the time I didn't know what better to do than to call it a night. I gave up. I dropped onto the sand face first and breathed heavily. Particles of sand flew into the distance with the force of my thud. I thought if I fell asleep, I would be back home when I woke up. This nightmare would be over, and I could erase it from my memory. I tossed and turned and forced my eyes closed until I couldn't do it anymore. Sleep never came. I heard a rumbling in the distance. I hoped it was thunder because that would mean that a storm was coming. I waited for a long while. Rain never came. I got back up on my feet. I would be damned if I was going to die here without fighting it out. I walked, fighting back tears from my eyes because I didn't have the water in my body to spare. I took three steps, and I couldn't go any further. I fell back onto the sand and rested. Sleep finally came.

When I slept, I had dreams about things that I had witnessed recently. I dreamt about Jenna sleeping with a smile on her face. I dreamt of hearing her speak in her smiley voice. I dreamt of my mother being calm in the hospital waiting room. I dreamt of my father in the hospital gown, and I woke up. It wasn't the image that startled me; it was the fact that I had all these people to get back to and I was lying there asleep, drooling in the sand. I opened my eyes and looked up and saw that the sun was coming up. I didn't know how long I slept for, and I had no idea what time it was and I didn't care. I was going to make it out of that wasteland and go back to Jenna. I had to do it for her smile. I had to go back for my parents; they needed me now more than ever. I had just gotten the best job in the world, and I had barely even gotten any work done. When I was asleep, I had swallowed some sand. I spat out the leftover bits that were still in my mouth and stood up. I dusted the sand off myself and took a step forward.

'Not so fast.' I heard from behind me.

I turned around and saw the frame of a man that was well over six feet tall. I couldn't see his face, or any other part of his body for that matter, because he was fully covered from head to toe. He had a black robe that covered his entire upper body, sort of like a ninja, with a cape that reached halfway down his back. He had a mask made with a thin fabric that covered everything but his eyes. If you looked closely, you could see through the fabric, but even if you did manage that, you couldn't see much. He was standing in front of hundreds of people that were wearing the same clothes. All of them were armed with assault rifles.

I held my hands up in the air and yelled, 'Don't shoot! I have no idea how I ended up here, please . . . please help me!'

The large man walked towards me. I took a step forward to meet him halfway. It turned out that that was a bad idea because each and every one of his men pointed their guns at me.

'On your knees!' one of them yelled while shooting his gun into the distance, making sure to just scare me and not scar.

I did as he ordered and looked away, scared for my life.

I heard the man's boots come closer, and soon enough, they came into my line of sight. He stopped walking a few feet away from me.

'Look at me,' the man said.

I looked up in his direction and squinted. The sun was in my eyes, and I couldn't make out much.

'Please. Stand up,' he said as he lifted me off the ground. I was face to face with the man who was clearly towering over me. I looked over at his men and noticed that they still had their guns pointed at me. He noticed the expression of fright on my face and turned towards them.

'Stand down, you fools!' he yelled, waving his hand frantically.

The men put their weapons down and stood at attention.

'When did you get here?' he asked.

'I . . . I, I don't know . . . I was in my office, and I shut my eyes. There was a ringing.'

'I do not care for how you came. I asked you when!' he yelled.

'Yesterday!' I mumbled. His voice was what I imagined terror would sound like if it had a voice.

'Where are those that you came with?'

'I didn't come here!' I yelled back. I noticed from his eyes that he didn't like to be spoken to that way. I didn't have much of a choice; I was staring down the barrels of a few hundred guns. 'I don't know who you are and what you want from me. I just want to go home!'

He took a step closer to me, and I got a good look at his eyes. They were as black as coal and as unforgiving too.

'There were others that came with you. We will find them,' he said as he walked back to his group. When he got to them, they separated into two files and cleared a pathway for him. He walked through the middle and got to the end; his army turned with him. The man turned around and looked into my eyes.

'Come,' he said.

I walked towards the sea of people and the path had been sealed. The formation had been remade, and they began to march behind their leader. I followed them closely.

I was a bit sceptical about following this man, but I didn't really have much of a choice. It was either stay there and feel the wrath of one hundred bullets being fired at me or go with them. I was beginning to slow down because my breathing was being challenged by the dryness of my throat. Someone in the back row of militia noticed this and yelled something that I couldn't decipher. I saw the giant of the man that was leading them in the distance raise his arm and the entire troop stopped in their tracks. The man that initially made the noise broke out of formation and came towards me. He handed me a flask of water.

'Drink,' he said as he waited for me to sip on it hungrily. I savoured each sip, and it got over far too soon.

'More,' I whispered, licking my lips.

He pulled out another flask from a small bag that he had slung on his back that I hadn't noticed before. Everyone in the group seemed to have one. I didn't question it. I just drank the water and handed him the empty flasks when I was done. He got back into his spot in the formation, and as though there was some unspoken language, the troop began to march forward. I marched behind them. I was no longer thirsty, and I was still alive. That's better than I was doing this morning.

We stopped after a few hours of walking and made camp. There were several fires lit and a few hundred tents pitched in a matter of minutes. Half the men had left the camp and gone somewhere. I found this odd but didn't probe further. I sat by myself by a fire and stared into it.

'Men believe that we all come from ashes and end up as ashes,' the giant of a man said as he took a seat next to me on the sand. I stopped and looked at him, unsure of whether I should stand up. 'Men do not know that we are born whole, the fire within us converts us into ashes.'

I didn't say anything.

'I am sorry about the way I treated you earlier. I am here to help you,' he said putting his hand on my shoulder. He wasn't even applying pressure on my shoulder, but he clearly didn't know his own strength. I winced a little, but he paid no heed to it.

'You see: these are my people. They are here because they support everything I stand for. They help me protect them by rendering their services to me. I take normal men and make soldiers out of them. My doors are open to whoever wants to aid the cause.' He stopped and looked out in the distance. 'What is your name?' he asked.

'Oliver Turner.'

'Oliver. My people say that I am an angel, but I do not believe it to be true.' He didn't say angel the way it would normally be said. He said it more like *Aa-ni-yell* I thought that was peculiar, but if I was going to ask him about something, it wouldn't be about his pronunciation.

'Your people?' I asked.

'Everyone you will meet from here on out are my people. That is of course, barring those you came with.' He fixed his gaze back on me.

'Look! You keep saying that I came here with people. I ended up here by myself. I didn't want to be here in the first place . . .' He cut me short and began shushing me.

'I have been told that you were not alone. You came with four more people. Two men and two women.'

'That's impossible!' I retorted. 'I was walking a whole day before you found me, and I'm pretty sure that I was walking alone.'

'That is where you are wrong, Oliver.' he said as he looked back into the distance. 'Man never walks alone.'

He stood up and dusted the sand off his body. 'My men will return with food for all of us. You will dine with us,' he said. It didn't seem like an offer; it felt more like an order. I was starving anyway, I wouldn't argue either way. I simply nodded my head.

'What is your name?' I asked before he walked away.

He turned back and smiled at me and said, 'I have many names, but my people call me Angel.' He said Angel in the same way as he did before; and then he continued, 'Tonight, after our meal, we will sleep, and then we will find your friends.'

Then he faded into the distance, and I was left sitting there alone by the flame, thinking about everything that Angel had just told me.

# NINE

## REUNION

I awoke atop a heap of sand. I didn't recall falling asleep, but I had been tired from all the walking. I remember eating alone by the fire; one of the guards bought me soup and some meat. I would love to have said that it tasted like chicken, but it wasn't. It was the desert though, and I was being held there against my will, so I wasn't really in a position to argue about my food preferences. After the meal, another guard gave me a clay glass filled halfway with a clear liquid. I declined it at first, but he insisted.

'Drink,' he said, looking down at me. 'It will help keep you warm.'

I kept it by my side and tried to fight the urge to drink. I was contemplative as to when I would be offered something to drink next, so I decided to drink it eventually. The air was starting to cool down as the heat from the sand below me flew upwards into the night sky; I had witnessed how unforgiving the desert could be at night, before I met up with Angel and his crew. If this drink did help with the cold, I would have to drink it. It was coarse and heady, and as I took a sip, I felt my throat burning up. It tasted like homemade vodka. It wasn't a tasty drink, but it was effective because no sooner did I put the glass down than I fell asleep, unbothered by the cold.

The fire by my side had sizzled to a halt. There was still steam coming out of the pyre on which it sat which indicated that I couldn't have been asleep for too long.

I took a moment to scan my surroundings and found that I was left there alone. The tents that had been made for the troops were all evacuated. I looked further into the distance and saw what appeared to be the whole group of men huddled in a circle. Curiosity got the better of me and I walked towards them.

There was silence like I had never heard before. I tried making my way through the crowd to figure out what was at the centre of this enormous circle. I heard a woman crying and a man, with an accent similar to mine, yelling at someone. I couldn't tell what it was that he was saying, but I had to get closer and find out more.

I pushed my way through the crowd and noticed that there was a man lying down in the sand while a woman sat by his side weeping. I looked closer and noticed that the man on the ground was my boss Mister Astiff; the woman weeping was his assistant Becky. I pushed harder and began to yell, 'Move! Let me through!' trying to get the guards to budge. I got as far as the front row, and three men broke out of formation and held me with the collar of my shirt. They started yelling at me in a language I didn't understand. Angel stopped them.

'Enough!' he yelled, and the guards dropped me down. 'Let him through,' he ordered.

I ran to where Mister Astiff's body lay and got to my knees. He was alive, but barely. He was breathing heavily, and he was losing colour.

'Get an ambulance!' I yelled, impulsively.

There was no response from anyone.

'Well? What the hell are you waiting for? Do it!' I urged.

While I was trying to get Mister Astiff to breathe, I felt a hand on my shoulder. I turned towards my back and noticed that it was Brad. He wasn't as energetic as he had been when we were together the last time, but a couple of days in the desert will do that to anyone.

'It's no use. I already tried,' he said.

'They just want him to die here!' Becky said, still weeping.

Francine came over from where Brad came through and sat by Becky's side.

'Francine?' I said, softly.

'It's the strangest thing,' Brad said to me, 'the last thing that any of us remember is being at that meeting, and the next minute we ended up in the middle of nowhere.'

'The same thing happened to me!' I was unsure what was going on, but in a way, I was glad that I had someone to share this experience with, someone that knew what I was going through.

'Did you guys all get here together?' I asked.

'No, but we were only a few feet away. Mister Astiff was the furthest away out of the lot of us. We had to do some walking to find him. When we did though, he was . . .' He paused and looked over at Mister Astiff lying flat on his back on the ground. 'Like this,' he finished.

'Now if you are done getting reacquainted. I believe we have some business to attend to,' Angel said from behind us.

Brad turned around and looked furious. He walked right up to Angel and started yelling, 'Look here, mister man, there is no way in hell that we are leaving our friend here to die in the desert! Do what you want with us after you've given him the help he needs!'

Angel was getting angry. You could tell because there was a vein in his forehead that was throbbing so hard it looked as though it would pop right through his skull.

He snapped his fingers and walked towards the biggest tent situated right in the middle of the other tents. The circle closed in on us, and the guards held out their guns and aimed at us.

'Walk,' one of them said while picking up Francine and Becky from Mister Astiff's side and hurling them towards Brad and myself.

He picked up Mister Astiff and put one of Mister Astiff's arms around his shoulder. He walked behind us as the circle parted, creating a pathway to the tent that Angel had just gone into.

I looked over at Brad who was biting his lower lip to the point that it was bleeding. I knew what he was thinking. Maybe he could take one or two guards out, but there were another hundred to deal with. He felt powerless, as did I.

We made our way to the tent. Mister Astiff was being dragged there on the shoulders of one of the armed men. We stopped right outside the tent. Angel came outside to greet us. 'Come,' he said as he walked back inside.

We were escorted into the room by three guards. The one leading the way had Mister Astiff on his shoulders, and the two others came in after we did.

The inside of the tent looked like a palace, as far as tents go. There were drapes all around the insides of the tent and a hole, neatly cut out, on one of the sides to form a makeshift window. There was a bed big enough for a giant, which was fitting because its owner was one, and a round metal table in the centre of the tent with six chairs around it.

'Sit,' he said, pointing out to the empty chairs.

We all sat down, reluctantly. The guard put Mister Astiff on one of the chairs. We all looked over to see how he was doing. He was still breathing heavily, but he was conscious.

I wanted to try and reason with Angel, try to get him to see that Mister Astiff would die at this table if he didn't get help. 'Mister Angel, sir, I . . .' I was cut short by Angel, who went on to say, 'Do you know the burden of leading one hundred men through the desert? They all rely on me for safety and provisions. I do it every day for decades! Then you come along stating that you don't know what you are here for and ruin the order that I work so hard to maintain.' He slammed his palm on the table. Becky and Francine had tears running down their eyes, and I could tell that they were having a hard time trying not to squeal.

'Mister Oliver, do you believe that there is a reason to everything that happens?' he asked.

I didn't have an answer to give him. I was unsure of whether there was anything that could justify this situation that had been thrust upon us. Even if I did have an idea of what to say, would it be what he wanted to hear?

Thankfully, I didn't have to find out because he answered his own question. 'Everything has a purpose. Even the five of you being out here, I don't know what your purpose is yet, and I am not going to stick around to find out. It is clear to me that you do not wish to stay here as much as I do not wish you to.' Angel paused for a moment and looked around the room. 'There is but one conclusion to draw from this, and that is that we must make an arrangement that is mutually beneficial to all of us. So let's see how I can help you.'

I looked over in complete dismay. I had already told him that we didn't come to his land willingly; neither of us knew how we had landed there in the first place. All we wanted was to go back home. I didn't see what was there to talk about because he wanted us to get out of his domain and we wanted to go back to ours.

As though reading my mind, he said, 'You all want to get back to where it is from whence you came.' He said, 'I will take you there, but along the way, I will make you amuse me in bizarre ways.' He laughed when he finished his sentence.

'You see, the desert is a boring place to live, and there is little, if not nothing, to do here to amuse oneself.' He continued, 'So I will get you home. In return, you will play some games.'

'We didn't sign up for any games!' Brad said, 'We're sorry to have wasted your time.' I looked over at my peers sitting around the spherical metal table that we were seated at and then at Mister Astiff who was struggling to stay alive. Brad signalled to all of us to get up and move out of the room. 'Thank you for your hospitality and getting us all together, but I think that we'll be fine on our own from here on out.'

'Not so fast . . .' Angel held up his index finger, keeping his gaze fixed on the centre of the table. The three men dressed in all black behind him came closer to the table and pointed their guns at us. 'You came to my land. You need help, and I wish to give it to you.' He paused, reaching to his hip. 'This right here is a far simpler gun than the ones you see my friends waving around,' he said as he put down a silver revolver on the table in front of us. The gun looked much older than the guns we had seen so far. The shiny bits of metal were beginning to give way to rust, and the entire nozzle had scratches on either side.

He unloaded the six bullets from the gun onto the table. The sound the bullets made when they hit the table is something that I won't soon forget. He picked up one of the bullets and loaded it into its chamber. 'Russian roulette is the game . . . and the stakes are high!' he said.

'I don't understand . . .' I began clearing my throat and continued, 'What's the need for this madness?'

'My dear friend, have I not helped you whenever you were in need?' he was spinning the revolver's cartridge, shuffling the whereabouts of the bullet. 'You lied to me and said that you came here alone, yet here you sit with four of your friends,' he said as he lay the gun back down on the table. 'I'm a bored man. I tire of the mundane far too easily for my liking. Don't get me wrong, I do like my life . . . It's just that, I'd rather have one of yours . . . Just for tonight.'

I was trying to decode his cryptic message. I knew this man was borderline insane, but this was crazy even for him. I knew what Russian roulette was; I had seen it in an old mafia movie a long time ago. One bullet enters the gun, participants take turns pointing the gun to the side of their temple and pulling the trigger. If the participant survives that round, the gun is passed around to the next person until one person finally wins a bullet to the brain. He was trying to make us earn our keep. He was the only one who seemed to have a grip on what was going on in this wretched place, and he was the only one with means to help get us back home.

'Let's just say there's one too many of you to get to where you are going. I could just ask my men to kill one of you at random, but that would not be enjoyable for me because I will not be the target of your hatred and that is a position I wish to hold for a little while. There are five of you here, and I can only move four. I have over a hundred men to lead into the night tonight and each one over that counts. The first one to die will not be coming on our trip.' Everything the man just said cleared all my doubts. My friends around the table were beginning to hyperventilate, but I'm sure they'd understand if I agreed to his terms. In my head, it was either die alone in this dreadful place or go home to my fiancé, my parents, my job at UTT, my old life. How could I take one of their lives without their consent? How could I say yes without consulting them? After all, there was no guarantee that I would make it out of there alive either.

'What if we say we don't need your help anymore?' I asked. I noticed my friends smiling, faintly, with relief. The colour had rushed back into their faces. At least now they knew that I tried negotiating.

The man picked up the gun from the table, stared at it for a while, and then swiftly held it out towards us. His finger rested on the trigger as he panned from left to right, pointing it at each of us. The room was filled with the sound of heavy breathing. Each person he pointed the gun at was more stoic than the person before him. No one wanted to look like a coward; we had endured too much to go out like that. We didn't want to give him the satisfaction. Just then he did something I never expected him to. He turned the gun towards himself, holding it to the side of his head with his finger on the trigger. He let out a loud yell and pulled the trigger.

*Click.*

He put the gun down hurriedly and snapped his fingers. One of the gunmen stationed behind him pulled out a handkerchief from his pocket and handed it to his boss. Angel wiped the sweat off his brow and tossed the napkin in the general direction of his employee.

'Say no again and I take a second turn,' he said with a sadistic smile developing on his lips. 'I must warn you though, I've played this game a thousand times . . . and yet, here I sit.'

'Could we have a minute to discuss it?' I asked, only because I wanted a few moments to think about my options. I didn't really need to discuss it with anyone. I just needed a minute to myself. Sadly, that was a minute I wasn't about to get.

The man slammed his hands on the table, causing the unused bullets to bounce to the ground, making that same bone-chilling sound they made earlier when he poured them onto the table. He yelled once more as he picked up the gun and put it to the side of his head.

*Click.*

He put the gun back on the table. 'Your turn,' he said.

# TEN

## GUN AND GAMES

The time had come for us to make a choice; the shame of it all was that the choice was already made for us. If we hesitated for another moment, Angel would take the gun to his head yet another time and possibly leave us with fewer choices or worse just order his men to shoot us all down one by one. The truth was that there were four shots left in that gun, one bullet and five of us. The odds were against us. One of us would die in that room. The question that was begging answering was—Who?

There were a few seconds that went by without anyone saying a word. Angel stared at each one of us for a few seconds each, waiting to see who would pick up the gun. We sat there staring at the gun on the table, hoping that the bullet in the chamber didn't have our names on it.

'I don't have all day,' Angel said. 'Either you make the choice or . . .' he was interrupted by Brad who picked up the gun from the table and held it to his head. He yelled as he pulled the trigger.

Becky gasped, her tears still flowing down her cheek in a steady stream. I couldn't believe what just happened.

*Click.*

Brad put the gun back on the table, and resting his head in his palms, he cried.

'Four people left, three shots to go,' Angel said with a wry smile. 'Who's next?'

72

I didn't think about it further. It wasn't a sure thing that the bullet would be waiting for the last shot to come flying out of the gun. Perhaps this shot would be the one that ended it. If so, at least this would all be over.

I picked up the gun and held it to the side of my head, thinking about Jenna, my parents, and everything that had ever been good in my life. I never knew what people meant when they said that at the time of death, your whole life would flash before your eyes until mine did. I pulled the trigger.

*Click.*

I had barely put the gun back down on the table, and Francine picked it up. She looked over at Becky. 'I'm sorry!' she said with tears in her eyes. She pulled the trigger.

*Click.*

Becky was shaking and sobbing wildly. Her time had come to pick up the gun. Five shots had been fired, there was one left.

She held the gun to her head, crying louder than before. She had trouble holding the gun straight because of how shaky her hands were. Brad didn't look up after he had taken his turn. I didn't look away from the gun, and Francine sat there staring into Becky's eyes, probably, wishing that she was the one that died instead of making Becky bite the bullet.

Becky cocked the gun and was about ready to pull the trigger. Just then the unthinkable happened. Mister Astiff heaved a loud sigh and reached for the gun from Becky's hands. He grabbed it and pulled it towards him almost instantly.

'No!' Becky yelled. But it was too late. Mister Astiff had pulled the trigger and taken the bullet.

Blood flew out of Mister Astiff's head, splattering evenly on all of us. Becky got the most of the splatter; a whole side of her face was drenched in the crimson hue of blood. If she was a wreck before, there was no defining the state she was in now.

Before any of us had a chance to process what had just happened, Angel clapped his hands.

'Excellent showing!' he said. 'Come now, we must begin our journey.'

Angel got up and walked out of the room followed by the guards. Brad was the first to follow, taking Francine with him. I stood up and looked over at Becky who was staring at the blood on her hands and then over at Mister Astiff.

'He took a bullet for me,' she said, not breaking her stare.

'I know,' I said, partly in disbelief. 'Come.' I lifted her off her seat and followed everyone else out.

Mister Astiff's motionless body was left in the room, the gun still in his hand.

When we had gotten out of the tent, we noticed a military-style truck parked just a few feet away from the camp, in the same spot where I had met up with my friends.

Angel was waiting for us outside the truck. He opened the rear door of the truck, and when we looked inside, we noticed it was covered in hay. It had three rather large dogs, Doberman I'd presume, and a woman dressed in the same outfit as Angel's men. The only way I could tell that she was a woman was because she was wearing the robes but not the veil. Her body was curvaceous, and her thick black hair was tied into a ponytail.

'Get inside. We will drive overnight and come daybreak. We will be outside the desert,' Angel said.

Neither of us had the energy to deal with anything at this point. We did as he said and got into the truck.

An armed guard walked in behind us and took a seat on one of the bales of hay.

The drive was bumpy. Becky had finally gotten a grip on things and had fallen asleep. Francine was staring blankly at the wall of the truck in front of her, and Brad was looking at the woman next to him.

'Keep your eyes to yourself,' the guard said to him.

Brad ignored his warning and tried speaking to the woman. 'What's your name?' he asked.

She turned away, as though she was afraid of him.

He tapped her on her shoulder, 'Hello?'

She turned away and curled up into a ball in the corner closest to her.

'It's no use,' the guard said. 'Our people are sheltered. They are scared of anyone who is new here.'

'Why?' Brad asked.

'Our people believe that whenever outsiders come to our land, they bring death with them.'

I didn't know what to make of that. They had a leader like Angel who killed people for fun, and yet they were afraid of death! It didn't add up in my head.

'Your people?' Brad asked.

It amazed me how calm Brad was about the events that had just transpired. It was something that I couldn't do. I didn't have the will to strike up a conversation. All I wanted to do was sit there and have a few moments to myself.

'Angel's people. We walk in the path that he guides us into, no questions asked,' the guard responded.

'She doesn't look too happy here,' Brad said while looking over at the woman in the corner. She turned her face towards Brad and looked him in the eyes. Her sky blue eyes were probably the prettiest I had ever seen. She shook her head from left to right grimly and looked away again.

'The welfare of our people is none of your concern,' the guard said while reaching for his gun. 'If you question our great leader in any way, I will consider it an act of treason and end you.'

'No, please. Don't!' Francine whispered. I had forgotten she was there the whole time; Francine had a way of going unnoticed. She had that effect on me in the meeting we had before we got here too. She would just be so still and quiet that she became easy to miss.

'I will not, for now,' the guard said. 'Let that be a warning.'

Brad didn't probe further. He just turned his head to the side and made a pillow out of a bale of hay. He rested his head on it and fell asleep. I noticed that Francine resumed looking at the wall in front of her and showed no signs of fatigue. I would have stayed awake for longer, but I just wanted the day to be over; I shut my eyes and followed Brad's lead.

I remember it being close to sunset when we had gotten into the truck, but I had no idea how much time had passed. I noticed that the truck had stopped a few times in the night but didn't bother waking up fully to investigate. It was only when we were stopped for an unusually long time that Brad had woken up.

'Guys! Wake up!' he said, shaking me up a bit.

We all woke up and dusted the hay of our heads. Other than Becky, Brad, and myself, there was no one in the truck. The dogs were nowhere in sight and neither was the woman we travelled with.

'Wh . . . Where are we?' Becky said, rubbing her eyes.

'No idea,' Brad said. 'But the doors are open, and Francine isn't here. Should we get out?'

Becky didn't wait to respond. She jumped out of the truck, and Brad and I followed.

I took my first step out of the truck and noticed that there was grass under my feet, moist grass. The desert was long gone. We were in some sort of woods now. Angel's men were all spread out doing their own thing, and the night sky had a bit of a cool breeze flowing through it.

Francine was sitting on the ground by the tyre with her knees close to her chest. She was plucking leaves from the ground and tossing them away.

'We're not in the desert anymore,' I noticed.

'Thank God,' Brad said, inhaling deeply. 'I missed the feeling of moisture.'

A guard walked up to us and said, 'Eat. Dinner.' He pointed at a large spread laid on a massive picnic table.

'Oh, I'm starving!' Brad said as he hopped along to where the food was. I picked Francine up and walked with her and Becky shortly after Brad had left.

We sat down on the table and began filling up our plates. There were four plates filled with almost charred meat, two plates with boiled vegetables, and one plate with what looked like tomato ketchup, but tasted like vinegar.

'The food here sucks!' Brad said, wolfing down his fourth piece of meat.

'Well, it's all we got, so I'm not going to complain,' added Becky.

I had taken some of the vegetables but none of the meat. I reached over for a piece and noticed that Francine's plate was empty.

'Aren't you going to eat?' I asked.

Francine shook her head from side to side.

'Oh cool. More for me,' Brad said, reaching for another piece of meat.

'Eat something, Francine,' I urged.

Francine looked around at everyone on the table and finally broke her silence. 'Remember those dogs in the truck with us?' she said.

'Yeah what about them?' Becky asked.

Francine didn't say anything but instead looked over at Brad who was eating some of the meat.

Becky quickly set aside her plate, and I was coming to terms with becoming a vegetarian.

'That's disgusting, Brad!' Becky said, sipping on some water.

'Didn't you say you weren't going to be picky?' he retorted. 'I'm hungry.' He continued eating.

This newfound information was enough to get me to lose my appetite. I stopped eating and got off the table.

Francine walked with me, and Becky was trying to talk some sense into Brad, who would not stop eating piece after piece of dog meat.

The guards didn't bother us at all. They just let us be by ourselves because they were sure that we had no idea where we were and where to go from there. Every now and then they would break up and see what we were up to, never pursuing us for wandering too far. I won't lie, I thought about making a run for it, but even if I did escape, where would I go? What would happen to Becky and Brad or Francine if they chose not to come with me? We had all witnessed someone we know die at the same table as us. We had all travelled through the night in the back of a truck with dogs and strangers with guns. We had all eaten dog meat for the first time. Well, almost all of us. The truth was that we had endured too much together to jeopardise any of it.

'It would be nice to be back home,' Francine said, breaking the silence.

'Home,' I said, trying to recall what it would be like if we made it out of here.

'Ice cream,' she said out of the blue.

'Ice cream?' I asked, puzzled.

'Yeah, that's the first thing I'm going to get when I get home. What about you?'

I only thought of Jenna the whole time. I missed her so much it was beginning to hurt. All I wanted to do was get back to her and hold her in my arms. I wasn't sure if things would ever go back to being the way they were before, but whatever the situation was, I knew that Jenna and I would be able to work it out.

'My girlfriend,' I replied.

'Ah, a woman. Must be nice to have someone waiting for you, worried about whether or not you're going to be home,' she said, staring into the distance.

I would've told her that it wasn't a nice feeling knowing that she had no idea what was going on. If the roles were reversed and Jenna had mysteriously disappeared, I'd be devastated. I'd spend every waking minute trying to figure out where she was. I knew in my heart of hearts that she was doing the same thing and it was killing me.

Brad came up to us and stopped our conversation. He got as far as three steps away from us and said, 'Angel wants to see us. Come quick.'

We followed him back to where Angel was standing.

Becky was already there, standing in front of Angel who was surrounded in a semi-circle by his guards. He was holding some sort of black box in his right hand.

The three of us walked and took spots next to where Becky was standing.

'They're here. Now what is it?' Brad said to Angel.

Angel took a step towards us and tossed the black device on the ground in front of us.

'What is it?' I asked.

'Remember how I said that you will trade favours to get back home?' Angel said.

The four of us stood still, staring at the box at our feet.

'This is one of those favours. I only need two of you to do this for me.'

'What is it?' I asked again, more assertive this time.

'There is a marketplace not far from here. Some people there have doubts about how I lead them. I do not encourage second guessing in my realm,' Angel said, looking at me in the eyes. 'I only need two of you to place this there and rectify the mistakes of these people.'

'Is this box going to make them start believing in you again?' Brad asked.

Angel laughed, 'You are so naïve. This is not a mere box. It is a device that can change lives, and it has the power to take them.'

Angel's cryptic conversation style was beginning to annoy me because he hadn't answered the question I had asked him twice already. I decided to ask him one final time, 'What the fuck is it?'

His smile and laughter faded, and he finally answered my question, 'It's a bomb. Two of you will plant it. You have ten seconds to tell me which two of you will go.'

# ELEVEN

## FLAMES

'**A**re you crazy? You can't expect us to blow a whole marketplace up?' I said in disbelief.

'It would be in your best interest to not pick a quarrel with me, young man,' Angel said. His tone was stern.

'I'll do it,' Becky said.

'Good. At least someone in this group has some form of sense. Who will go with her?' he asked.

There was a stunned silence among the rest of us. I hadn't fully recovered from watching my boss die before my eyes and, selfishly, I was hoping that someone else from the group would volunteer. I looked down solemnly at my feet and said nothing. Even without looking up, I noticed Becky staring at me.

'No volunteers?' Angel said, and then continued, 'You'll have until the sun comes up to decide who goes with the woman. This is a two-person job, and the chances of success are a lot higher if one of you goes with her. Of course, things being the way they are, I will send her out on her own if none of you come forward.' He stopped and looked over at Becky and then said, 'Prepare yourself. You have chosen your own fate.' He walked away and his crew of mercenaries followed suit. We were left standing besides two guards who guided us into what appeared to be an abandoned building on the far side of the table where we sat to eat dinner. I hadn't noticed any form of civilisation until I saw that building, but that was easy to miss considering that it was dark that night and that the building was made of unpainted cement. I hadn't the faintest idea as to why we were being led there because the building looked like it had survived an explosion, albeit barely. It stood in front of us, a two-storey building, but by looking at it, you could tell that there used to be more floors, once upon a time. There were cracks running along the side of the building and open cut-outs where windows used to be. There was a sheet of metal resting on framework that once belonged to a door of some sorts. One of the guards pulled aside the metal with great difficulty, and the other one nudged us inside. There was no resistance from either of us. We just wanted to be alone, at least I did.

When we got in, the guards placed the metal back on top of the opening and sealed us shut. When we walked in, we went our separate ways exploring our surroundings. At first glance, I thought the building was a dump. Upon closer inspection, I learnt that my suspicions were right. There was nothing in the room, just empty open spaces with pillars on the sides; some made it to the roof while others didn't. When I say roof, I'm using the term loosely; there wasn't really a roof, just wooden planks running from one pillar to the other, with cracks in between them. If you stood at the right spots, you could see the night sky overhead. There was a metal trash can in the centre of the room; it had a high flame jutting out of it. When I had visited New York one winter with Jenna, she had spotted out a few homeless people huddled up around a similar fire.

'Isn't it sad to see people spend Christmas like that during the holidays?' she had said to me.

'What, warm?' I joked.

'No silly!' She punched my shoulder playfully. 'Out in the cold all alone with no place to put a Christmas tree.'

'You can't be responsible for everyone, babe. People make choices, and sometimes those choices don't work out so good.'

When I was in New York, I saw the situation differently, but now, as I sat in an empty room with nothing but a fire in a trash can and three people I barely even knew, I thought about what I had said then.

*People make choices and sometimes those choices don't work out so good.*

What choices had I made that made me end up here? Unknowingly, I had walked close to the trash can and held my hands up over the flame. Brad came up beside me and started doing the same thing.

'He's going to kill us all,' he said, without breaking his gaze from the fire.

I didn't say anything. In my mind, I hadn't ruled that out as a possibility, but all that I had keeping me going was the hope that maybe we could make it. Maybe all of us could meet over coffee and talk about the obstacles that we had overcome. It was a long shot, but it was all I had.

'You know it too, right?' he asked, finally staring up from the fire.

'If he wanted to kill us, we'd already be dead,' I said as I walked away towards an empty corner of the room.

'Think about it for a second,' Brad said a lot louder this time. 'The gun game with Robert, the whole bomb thing tomorrow.' He paused after learning that he didn't just have my attention; he also had the attention of Francine and Becky who were sitting next to each other on one side of the room. He cleared his throat and continued, 'He wants us to kill ourselves. I don't know why exactly, but I'm sure it turns him on. He's a sick motherfucker, and he gets hard when he sees people kill themselves!'

Becky was crying. She was trying to be discreet about it, but with Becky's emotions, when it rained, it poured.

'Brad . . . that's enough,' Francine said, holding Becky's hand.

'None of us are making it out of here alive,' he said softly.

Becky had now begun crying hysterically.

'Stop it, Brad!' Francine yelled.

'It's the truth! You'll see.'

When he said that, I looked over at Becky and noticed something. There wasn't sadness in her eyes . . . I could see that she was overcome with emotions but sadness wasn't one of them. Her eyes expressed a feeling that I could relate to, the only feeling that I had felt ever since I woke up in the desert. Fear.

Then it hit me. Becky wasn't sad or afraid of what Angel wanted. Becky had signed up to go and blow up a market. Brad saying the things he was saying must've cleared any doubt that she was having about making it out of there alive.

I walked over to Brad and whispered in his ear, 'Bomb.'

He looked up from the fire and then at me, confused for a moment, but I could tell that he understood what I was trying to convey eventually.

He walked over to Becky and took a seat besides her.

'I'm sorry, Beck. I'm . . . I'm an idiot,' he said.

Becky put her head on Brad's shoulder and began sobbing. Brad continued apologising and consoling her. It seemed to be working. Francine stood up from where she was sitting and came and stood next to me.

'She's too weak to go through with it on her own, Ollie,' she said to me.

'I know.'

'I'm going to go with her,' she said. I looked at her in complete dismay. I had secretly hoped that someone would volunteer and that I would get a free pass out of this whole mess, but when the moment came, I didn't feel relieved. Instead I felt distraught. I wanted to butt in, but she realised it and continued talking.

'Just promise me something.' She looked into my eyes. I could see the reflection of the fire in her pupils. 'Take your girlfriend for ice cream when you get out of this.' She walked away and sat down.

The fire began dying down, and each of us found a comfortable spot to lie down in. Brad fell asleep with Becky on his shoulder, and I couldn't tell from the angle and because of the darkness that was suddenly creeping up on the room whether or not Becky was still awake, but she wasn't crying anymore, so I felt some relief.

I looked down into the trash can and saw the final embers burn out. Then I thought about what Jenna had done that night in New York.

'Come with me,' Jenna said as she dragged me to the fire where the homeless people were huddled up. I followed her, curious enough to find out what she wanted to do to comply without questioning. She squeezed through creating enough room for the two of us to get in between the people already standing over the fire. The people didn't fight her, instead welcomed her. It amazed me to see that people with so little were willing to share anything, even the little scraps that they had to make do with. Jenna smiled and looked at me and then to the person on her right. She held his hand and with her other hand held mine. The man next to her held the hand of the person next to him, and I did the same with the woman next to me. A few seconds before, we were just strangers passing by, but in that moment, as we circled a fire holding hands, we weren't strangers, we weren't acquaintances, but something more . . . we were one person.

With whatever little light there was, still aflutter from the dying fire, I spotted Francine and noticed that she had fallen asleep where she sat down, by herself in the corner, and I couldn't bear to keep that image in my mind in the event that she didn't make it back when the sun came up and the deed was done. I found a place to sit beside her and held her hand. I thought about how Jenna had smiled at me when she noticed that I had felt the same way she did about that moment and thought about what she would think at this moment. If somehow, someway, she had seen me following in her footsteps, I knew that she would be smiling now. That night I fell asleep with a smile on my face knowing that I had made Jenna smile. It wasn't real; it was just a hope and a dream, but that was enough to get me through the night, through the next day and back into her arms. Hope was all I had; I wasn't ready to part with it just yet.

I had dreamt of Jenna in the desert, and I had thought about her every minute that I was awake thereafter, but that night, I didn't have a single dream. It was a blissful slumber nonetheless. I wish the same could be said about my awakening.

The metal door was pushed aside and then tossed to the ground, causing a thud so loud that the four of us woke up instantaneously. Becky and Brad got up to their feet before Francine and I had even woken up properly. When Francine noticed that I was holding her hand she looked at me and smiled. I hadn't had the time to get to know Francine when we were in the UTT together but I had come to regret it. I knew that if the circumstances had been any different we could have been great friends. Maybe even more like brother and sister. She patted my hand and rose to her feet. I followed her lead.

Angel walked through the doorway; his frame was so large that he had to bend down to enter inside. He stood in front of the door, thus almost sealing out all the light coming from behind him. Luckily for us there were cracks in the roof, so we could see clearly.

'You,' he said, looking at Becky, 'it is time.'

Becky walked next to him; the fear in her eyes had gone.

'Have you come to a decision as to who will accompany your friend?'

Francine began to take a step forward, but I couldn't let her go through with it.

'Yes,' I said, 'I'll go with her.'

Becky looked over at Brad, and Francine looked over at me. Just by those exchanges it was clear to me, Francine had told me she would go with Becky and Brad had told Becky that he would accompany her. I couldn't just sit there and get a free ticket back home after all. Jenna wouldn't like if I had.

'Good. Come with me.' He walked out of the room, bending down again, and we followed him outside. Once we were outside, Becky turned around to see Brad and Francine one more time before the guards lifted the door and put it back in place. I didn't turn around. I didn't want to look back. I just wanted to get this ordeal done with as quickly as possible.

Angel took a few steps ahead towards the dinner area and stopped when he reached a car.

It was a beaten up silver sedan. I couldn't tell what make it was because the paint had come off it and some parts had been consumed by rust. It was quite perplexing to look at because it didn't look like an old car; in fact, it looked newer than the car I drove. But there it stood, beaten up and downtrodden.

'Get inside,' Angel said, opening the driver's side door. I walked over to it without consulting Becky, and she opened the door to the passenger seat and climbed in shortly after me.

When I got inside, I noticed that there was a hole where the speedometer used to be, creating a window into the engine. There was a GPS screen to my right and a slot for a CD player, but there was something else in its place. It looked like a big clock. The time showed *0.02*.

I thought it was broken at first, but then I thought about other possibilities. Perhaps the owner didn't care to correct the time on the clock.

My doubts were quickly cleared by Angel who said, 'Take this car to the marketplace. Turn right when you hit the road and you should see it about two miles away.' He stopped talking and turned his attention to the GPS and then continued, 'This should help you get there. Just a heads up though . . . Don't try and stray away from the course it shows you. The bomb will go off if you make one wrong turn.'

'Okay,' I said, nodding, trying to hide the fear in my voice. 'Where's the bomb?' I asked.

He smiled at me. 'It is no longer in the suitcase you saw earlier. We have changed its location to a more . . .' he paused as though adding weight to his sentence, 'convenient place.'

Angel had a way with words; he knew exactly how to evade answering any of my questions directly. I felt the need to clarify.

'Where is it?'

He chuckled and finally responded, 'You're in it.' He said, 'Now go!'

He shut the door and left us thinking about what he had just said. Becky stared into my eyes. I could see the fear in hers building its way back up.

I tried to turn the ignition on, but the car wouldn't start. Instead it just beeped. *Ding!*

Becky looked at me confused, and I tried again. I was hoping to hear the engine this time, but it wouldn't come on. *Ding!* It went again.

I looked out of the window and over at Angel who laughed a little bit before he began making some sort of gesture and began yelling the word, 'Seatbelt.'

I put my seatbelt on and turned the key sideways.

There was no ding this time, instead I heard a click and noticed the clock had gone from *0.02* to *0.01*. The engine started shortly after.

'I could have sworn that clock was a minute ahead before we started the car.'

She noticed it too. So it wasn't my mind playing tricks on me. But if that wasn't a clock, then what was it? I looked over at Becky who thought that she was clearly going insane and then I decided to think out loud so that she would have some company along the way to crazy town.

'If that's the timer to the bomb, it would have blown up already,' I said.

'Well, we haven't, so it's got nothing to do with the bomb?' Becky asked.

'I'm not sure. That click . . .' I began thinking of the clicking sound the car made before it started. I could've sworn it came from the clock.

'The sound that the clock made when you started the car? Try it again and see if it happens,' she said.

I put my hand on the key and almost did as she said and then it hit me.

'Becky . . .'

'Yes, what is it?'

'Every time the ignition is turned on, the clock ticks down.'

She looked at me confused. 'So the next time we start it . . .'

'The clock will be 0.00,' I said.

'That means . . .' she paused, 'the next time we start this car . . .'

I interrupted, 'Will be the last time.'

# TWELVE

## IGNITION

After driving on the dirt road for a few feet, a lady's voice came from the GPS device.

*'Take the next available right turn,'* it said.

I was instructed by Angel not to stray off course or the bomb that we were sitting on would blow up. I didn't think he was bluffing, and even if I did, I would not call him on that bluff. I took the right as directed and kept my eyes fixed on the GPS. We were on the right track. I sighed deeply, and Becky did too. One wrong turn could blow us to smithereens.

We kept going straight down the tarmac road and saw the market in the distance. When Angel said marketplace, I was expecting a whole civilised world with buildings and a whole lot of people. Instead what I was instructed to stop at by the kind GPS lady were ruins. It may have been a market once, but it stood in front of me mounds of dirt, rock, and brick. I turned the car off and sat there sullenly.

I pictured what the market would look like in its glory days—narrow cobblestone pavements with stalls on either side, sand under the stalls. The docks were just behind the market, so there was a narrow stretch of beach in the background. If such a place existed in Toronto, then that's where I'd do all my shopping. I imagined that there was a lot of hustle and bustle here during its peak.

Today, the stalls were just piles of rubble. The cobblestone was in tatters, and the dock behind the market was just a place where ships came to die a slow death by rust.

Vendors sat next to the rubble on an old bed sheet that they spread on the ground and sold anything from onions to dog meat. There were about seven such makeshift stalls and about eight people shopping from them in total. Why Angel wanted to blow this place up was beyond me; it was already ruined.

Before I had time to think about what his motives were, Becky got out of her seat and then walked around the car and opened my door. I sat there wondering what she was up to.

'Start the car and run!' she said to me.

'Let's just think about this!' I said, 'If I turn the key and the clock goes to 0.00, what do you think is going to happen?'

'You'll make it out! Just do it!' she yelled.

'No, I can't take the risk of killing you with me. Step away from the car!'

'Ollie, just turn the key. If it goes off, we're in this together.' There was something reassuring in her voice.

'I refuse to let you die with me, back off!' I pushed her away gently causing her to stumble and fall back. I turned the key and waited for the engine to come on. They say your whole life flashes before your eyes moments before your death. That was not the case in this instance. That was because I wasn't done yet. The engine didn't come on.

Becky looked at me as if she knew something that I didn't.

I got out of the car and lifted the hood. The engine was shiny and new. It was kind of oxymoronic to look at the car and then at the engine. You'd expect some rusty old heap of metal to be under the hood, but there was this gorgeous piece of engineering just sitting there under a ton and a half of rust. Becky got into the driver's seat and started fidgeting around with controls. Nothing changed. The car still wouldn't start. I told Becky to turn the ignition after I had discovered that there was nothing wrong with the engine.

*Ding!*

That instant I thought of Angel gesturing me to put the seat belt on. I knew Becky had made the connection too. The car wouldn't start without the driver's seat belt being fastened.

I slammed the hood shut and ran towards the driver's side door.

'Becky, no!' I yelled as I ran. I was too late. She was looking into my eyes when she did it, her seatbelt already fastened. She turned the ignition.

*Click.*

'Go,' she said.

It all happened too quickly. I remember looking at Becky's face, deep into her eyes. The fear was gone and had been replaced by a look of determination. She had known all along that she would be the one to blow that car up.

I took a few steps away from the car before it blew up, and the impact hurled me into the rubble. I heard screaming and the crackling of fire and felt a sharp pain on my head. The ringing in my ears had started again, more profound than the last time that I had encountered it. I couldn't take it anymore and shut my eyes and succumbed to the darkness.

Suddenly, I was back in the meeting room at the UTT, replaying the images of what happened when I first landed up in the desert.

*Brad was getting impatient, the way he'd always get when he was made to sit for too long. He began to interrupt anything that anyone was saying. Henry and Mitch weren't fazed by this and went on dealing with the situation calmly. Their calmness was making Mister Astiff livid because he had no control over the matter, and he hated not being in control. Francine just sat there chewing her nails, and as for me, I was sitting there trying to shut out the mind-numbing ringing in my ear.*

*When the yelling was almost insufferable, Becky walked in.*

*'Not now, Becky!' Mister Astiff yelled.*

*'Mister Jacoby is on line two for you,' she said. 'He said it's urgent.'*

*The yelling didn't die down at all. Brad kept hurling ideas at Henry and Mitch, and the two of them were just shutting down everything that Brad threw at them. Francine sat there chewing her nails. Mister Astiff kept ignoring everything that Becky was saying and yelling at the two suited men in front of him. Becky kept cutting in reminding Mister Astiff that there was a call for him, but she remained ignored.*

*All this wasn't even half as painful as the ringing. Oh that damn ringing! I couldn't take it anymore. I shut my eyes and covered my face, until all that there was, was darkness and that painful ring, a ring so sharp and loud that it made my head rattle. I pressed my fingers into my eyes trying to feel something, anything but that incessant ringing. Finally, the ringing got so loud that it felt as though it couldn't get any louder.*

*Then it stopped.*

*There was silence. I moved my hands and opened my eyes. I had to squint because there was a sharp light coming at me from all directions. While my eyes readjusted, I snapped my finger next to my right ear to see if I could hear it. I could; it still worked. When my eyes finally readjusted, I looked around and found that I was standing in the middle of a desert. There was nothing but sand under my feet for miles and miles. I was still wearing my black shirt and trousers. My hair was just the way it was this morning, but my wallet wasn't in my pants back pocket where it usually was. It was warm but breezy. Brad, Francine, Mister Astiff, Becky, Henry, and Mitch were nowhere in sight. Mister Astiff's office couldn't have just magically transformed into this! It was all too real to be a dream and yet there was no explaining it.*

*One minute, I was in a heated meeting, and the next minute, I found myself in the middle of nowhere.*

I kept trying to open my eyes to see if the ringing stopped. I couldn't tell where I was, but I could tell that I was being carried somewhere. I looked around trying to make sense of it, but I couldn't. Everything was hazy. I could see glimpses of sky and the sun in my eyes. I could hear people saying something in an alien language accompanied by the faintest ringing sound. Then it all stopped.

When I woke up, I saw that I was in some sort of a stretcher in what looked like an infirmary somewhere in Angel's camp.

Angel was sitting by my side and looking at me with a pained expression.

'You barely survived that explosion,' he said.

'Becky . . .' I whispered.

Angel shook his head.

I shut my eyes and let a tear fall out. *It should have been me in that driver's seat* if only I had remembered that the seat belt needed to be fastened.

Angel had stood up from his seat and put his hand on my shoulder.

'This isn't over,' he said. 'There is more that I will ask of you and the time to ask is coming upon us.'

'Why are you doing this?' I asked.

'I have no idea what it is you speak of,' he replied. 'All I am doing is giving you choices, and the ones you make impact the lives of those and the others with you. In fact, to highlight this for you, I will give you one more choice. But first you must meet up with your friends.' He walked out of the room and two guards came to my bedside. They picked me up by my shoulders and urged me to my feet. I hadn't recovered fully, and my feet were wobbly. It was hard walking straight, but with the support of the guards, I managed it.

They took me back to the torn down building where they were holding us earlier and pried open the metal door. I walked in, limping, and Brad and Francine came running up to me.

'Becky?' Francine asked.

I shook my head and looked down at my feet.

Brad began pacing the room. 'No! This . . . No! It can't be!' he said.

Francine put my arm around her shoulder and helped me into a corner of the room. I sat down, and she sat down beside me. Brad was still pacing, scratching his head and mumbling something to himself.

Angel walked into the room, and Brad charged at him.

'You bastard!' he said, running towards Angel.

Three gunmen by Angel's side yelled something that I couldn't decipher and raised their guns at Brad. He stopped in his tracks and smiled at Angel.

'I'll kill you, I swear,' he said.

Angel didn't acknowledge that threat.

He pulled out a pistol from his hip and slid it on the ground towards the trash can in the centre of the room.

'No, no more games, you sick fuck! This ends tonight!' Brad said.

'I suggest you calm down before you and your friends die a slow and painful death at the hands of my men,' Angel replied.

Brad looked at Francine and myself and thought better than to put us all at risk.

'We will move tomorrow. We will be closer to where it is you need to go, and I assure you that you will get whatever it is that you seek. But two is company and three is a crowd.'

'What does that mean?' Francine asked, standing up from next to me, stopping to make sure if I was okay to sit on my own. I was.

'I will grant one wish to whoever uses this gun. There is a catch though. After I complete your wish, you will shoot yourself and no one else.' He took a step towards the door and then turned back around to finish what he was saying, 'I will leave the door open today, and my men and I will be stationed just outside for when you come to a decision.

'Bring Becky back and I'll shoot myself,' Brad said without giving any of us to discuss it.

'I cannot do that, you ignorant fool!' Angel said, losing his composure. 'Don't play games with me. I don't take kindly to it. Any requests that have no way of being completed will be a grave mistake. I am giving you all a chance to get closure. Don't ruin it by insulting me.' He walked out of the room and left us alone.

Brad came over to the corner where I was sitting and took a seat next to me, covering his face with his hands.

'I have nothing to live for. My job is gone, my friends are gone, and now Becky . . .' Brad said solemnly. 'I'll do it. I'll ask for the guarantee of your safety.' He looked over at Francine and me.

'You can't. He won't entertain that kind of request,' Francine said to him.

I nodded. I knew that Angel was far too smart to let anything come in the way of all the fun he was having. Francine realised it too.

'I won't let you guys take the bullet. If no one comes forward by morning, I'll figure something out.' Brad walked away and lay down on the far side of the room. Francine took a seat next to me.

'In a perfect world, you could ask to be with your girlfriend and take the bullet yourself,' she said.

'That would be a perfect world. Die to be with the one person in the world who means something to me.'

'Well, you've already cheated death so many times to get to her. It would be a shame if you didn't make it,' she said.

'I'll take the bullet,' I said.

Francine looked at me confused. 'Why would you do that?' she asked.

'When I saw Becky die today in that car, it should have been me. I was the one in the driver's seat and I got out of it. I won't let anyone take my place again. I'm sure of it.'

Francine just smiled and a tear rolled down her cheek. 'You say things like that after knowing that you have more to live for than anyone of us. You don't understand, do you?' She paused. 'Our jobs, our careers, it took everything from us. None of us had anything to live for outside of the UTT. You do. We can't let you be the one to take the fall every time. You did with the bomb in the car. You were one of the first to take the gun to your head when Angel put it on the table.' I cut her off, 'Brad was first.'

'Yes, but that's because he's hyperactive and impulsive. You put thought into it. You calculated and figured out that according to statistics, that bullet should have had your name on it. You've already cheated death twice. You won't have to again,' she said.

I looked in the other direction; I didn't want her to see me cry. It was weird to hide my emotions after all that we had been through together, but I didn't want anyone to think less of me. I had cheated death more than once and didn't show any pain, but a few kind words were all it took to start the water works.

'Ice cream,' I said, trying to change the topic.

Francine smiled. 'Ice cream,' she said.

'What's up with that?' I asked.

'When I was younger, about ten or twelve years old, my dad would take me out for ice cream late at night. It became a tradition, like a bedtime story. Every day before going to bed, he would take me out for ice cream. When I was sixteen, he died, and I lost all desire to have it without him. I've gone a decade without it, and I just . . . miss him now more than ever.' She looked in the other direction. We were so much alike, Francine and me. We were brave in the face of adversity but deep down inside, we were suckers for mushy subjects.

'You'll eat it again soon,' I said. 'When we get out of this mess, you, Jenna, and me . . . we'll go get some ice cream.'

'Sounds like a plan,' she said.

Brad had gotten up and came sprinting towards us. He kneeled down in front of us and hugged us hard. Francine and myself were taken by surprise, but we returned the hug. It felt nice to share that moment because just like that night in New York with Jenna when I had realised that we were all one person, I felt that oneness with my colleagues. They were more than colleagues this moment. They had stared down the gullet of adversity and come out victorious. They had beaten the odds. They were just like me.

'In case I don't see you guys tomorrow, I just want you guys to know that there are many things I would have done differently. If I had known that this was how it would pan out, I'd never take the job at UTT.' He paused and broke the hug, and then he continued, 'Even still I don't regret it because I met you guys there. All of you, Robert and Becky . . . You guys.'

Francine shushed him and cut him off, 'We still have tonight. Only one of us has to die tomorrow.'

'That's what I came here to tell you guys. I'm going to do it when Angel comes to us at sunrise. I'll tell him to give you guys clean clothes and proper food, no dog meat,' he said.

'You'd die for clean clothes and a hot dog?' I asked.

'No, but I would die so that the two of you could live,' Brad said.

He went back into his corner and shut his eyes. Francine looked over at him and thought about what he had said. She turned around shortly after and said, 'Goodnight.'

The night was many things . . . Good was not one of them.

There were three of us here today, and in the morning, there would be one less. I had already let Becky die because I was given a choice and I made the wrong one. When morning came, I would beat Brad to it. I would take the bullet. Clean clothes and food weren't worth dying for, but people that would die for me . . . They were worth doing it for.

I had one night of sleep left; I had one last chance to see Jenna, even if it was just in a dream. I was not going to waste it. I shut my eyes and fell asleep. I was tired and drained from the whole bomb escapade. Sleep came easily.

I did dream of Jenna that night, and I thought of that night at *Uncle Mario's*. I could have sworn that I was sleeping with a smile on my face, because I had already gotten my last wish. The food and clothes for my friends was just a bonus.

The smile was wiped off my face quickly as I was rudely awoken by the sound of a gunshot somewhere in the distance.

Someone had beaten me to it.

# THIRTEEN

## FRESH WOUNDS

When I heard the gunshot, I was sure that Brad had done what he said he would. I looked up above through the cracks in the ceiling, the stars were still out which meant that whoever it was that pulled the trigger was in a hurry to get it done.

I noticed Brad was already up on his feet standing in the corner where Francine had fallen asleep. He was standing still which was unlike him. But if he was standing there and someone had in fact died, then it could only be one person.

I walked up to the corner where he stood, painfully, because I had not recovered completely from the explosion. My feet were still wobbly, and I needed to hold on to the walls for support. I managed it as best I could.

'I don't believe it,' Brad said in complete dismay.

My mind was telling me to look away, not to see what Francine had chosen to do because I was sure that it would break me. The only person that I made a connection with on this whole journey had killed herself and I would have to see her bloody remains in the corner of the room.

There was no blood. There was no body. There was no Francine.

All that sat in that dry corner was an empty bucket of ice cream.

Brad walked away and said to himself, 'She died for nothing.'

I stood there staring at the bucket of ice cream, knowing that she didn't die for nothing. She didn't die for the ice cream. She died for us.

Angel came into the room with two bags in either hand. He dropped it on the ground in front of his feet.

'What now?' Brad said. He didn't fight him the same way that he had been all these days. It sounded almost as though he had given up.

'Your friend drives a hard bargain,' Angel replied. 'She asked for clean clothes for the both of you, a feast tonight, and a bucket of ice cream for herself.' Angel began walking out of the room. He stopped before he got outside the door and added, 'No dog meat, I promise.'

Brad yelled at Angel to stop. Angel did.

'We want to eat now,' Brad said.

Angel stood there, contemplative for a second. 'As you wish,' he said.

I fought the weakness I was feeling and got up to my feet.

'Why not save the feast for dinner?' I asked.

'The wound is still fresh. You want it to heal as quickly as possible,' he said.

I instantly realised that he was talking about Francine's death. If she did, in fact, die for this meal, then we would have it while the memory of her was still fresh. I was on board with the idea because I was hungry anyway. I had been so tied up with Angel's demands that I had forgotten to keep tabs of what I had or hadn't been eating.

Brad put his arm around my shoulder and helped me walk out the door with Angel. Our usual spot in the camp was laid out for us. Angel wasn't kidding when he said that he had prepared a feast for us.

The table had a nice-clad picnic tablecloth laid out over it. There were no lights in the area, so every table there had candles on it. What every table didn't have, however, was a roast chicken set in the centre with sides of bacon and mash potatoes. There were boiled peas in a ceramic bowl and a dish filled with garlic bread. Brad and I were instantly drawn to the food. A little bit of drool dripped out of the corner of my mouth.

'All this food for just the two of us?' asked Brad.

'Five of us,' I corrected, looking over at the empty seats where Francine, Becky, and Robert would have sat if they were still here.

Brad looked away into the distance.

Angel came to the table with a tray that had three bronze goblets on it. He set it down on the table and took a seat next to us.

'We don't have alcohol here, but we make do with whatever we can,' he said. He also added, 'This is not a day of mourning, but a day of celebration. When life passes on, my people, we celebrate it. We embrace it.' He picked up a goblet and poured a little of the contents inside onto the surface of the earth by the table. It seemed like a fitting thing to do at the time, so Brad and I did the same.

'I will leave you two alone now,' Angel said. 'You can rest tonight. I promise to get you home tomorrow.'

He left the table shortly after having said it.

'Home,' Brad said, unsatisfied.

'Home,' I said, smiling.

'What the hell do I have left to go back to?' added Brad.

'What are you talking about?' I asked, puzzled.

'Nothing will be the same,' he said. 'You know that, right?'

I didn't know what to think at this point. I wasn't doing any of the things I had done for me. I was doing it to get back home to my normal life, to my girlfriend, and to my family.

'We didn't come all this way for nothing,' I said, picking up the goblet and drinking. It was the same drink they had given me on my first night. Once again I felt the same burning sensation when I swallowed and the irrefutable numbness that the drink provided. It wasn't alcohol, but it would do.

'What did we come here for?' Brad asked.

I said nothing.

Brad picked up a piece of chicken and put it on his plate. 'I don't think I can go back to a normal life after what I've just endured,' he said, reaching for some peas.

'I think I could use a little bit of normalcy,' I said.

I had tried to keep calm through it all. I could feel my sanity slowly slipping away, but I tried very hard to not let insanity take over. Brad had no problems letting his grip loose. He said, 'I don't even know what normal is anymore. Back home, I'd expect someone to die with every step I take.'

Somewhere deep down I knew that I'd be the same way for a while. I had gotten so used to chaos and death that I was starting to become immune to it. *Nothing, a few days with Jenna won't fix.*

Brad finished cleaning up a piece of chicken before he said, 'It seems like just yesterday, we had a full table. And now . . .'

I raised my goblet. Brad looked over at me, doing the same, and I said, 'To those we lost.'

'To those we lost,' Brad reiterated.

Brad and I kept eating for what felt like a long while. Either the food was really good or eating dog meat made us appreciate chicken that much more. The food on our table never seemed to run out, and Angel and his men saw to it that it never did. Every time we finished our drink or our plates were empty, one of the mercenaries would come and refill it for us.

I pushed my plate aside having eaten my full. 'What now?' I asked.

Brad smiled and picked up his glass, and then he said, 'Now we drink.'

# FOURTEEN

## Plain and Simple

I don't recall falling asleep that night, but I woke up on the chair that I had fallen asleep on. Brad wasn't on his chair; instead he had found a comfy spot on the grass below the table.

He came to his senses shortly after I did.

'What the hell happened last night?' Brad asked, getting up from under the table. He didn't quite know where he was because when he got up, the top of his head collided with the bottom of the table causing a loud thud.

'One too many drinks,' I said, trying to get to my feet.

I noticed that the weakness that had ailed me ever since the bomb incident had vanished. *Maybe alcohol can cure all wounds.*

Brad and I barely had time to make sense of things before Angel came to us, happy and upbeat.

Whenever Angel was happy, someone paid for it with their life. That wasn't a good sign.

'Good morning, friends,' he said, forcing emphasis on the word 'friends.'

'Morning!' Brad said, crawling out from under the table.

'Today, we will take you home,' he said, walking away from the table. 'Come,' he added.

Brad and I looked at each other, slightly dazed from the hangover, confused.

Angel walked up to the cargo car he had transported us in after he made us play Russian roulette.

'Get inside,' he said, opening the back door. We did as he asked.

Getting in the back of that car brought back some memories that I wish I hadn't recalled. The last time I got in the back of that van, I had three people with me. I would have had four, but I had witnessed one of those people offing themselves before my very eyes. All of that didn't matter now because I would be home. Angel promised that he would see us back to our normal lives if we had played his senseless games. We had survived everything he had managed to hurl our way. Broken, but somehow intact.

The door shut behind us, and we were immersed in darkness.

Brad didn't say much; I figured he was just nursing his hangover with a well-planned nap. I thought I'd do the same.

I tried to sleep, but I was too excited. Against all odds, today would be the day I finally saw Jenna again.

I pondered over what I would do when I finally see her again. I had envisioned several dozen scenarios, and each one of them sent my heartbeat aflutter and roused a smile on my face.

*My name is Oliver Turner. I spent the last few days cheating death, but today . . . Today, I reunite with my soul mate. Today . . . it was all worth it.*

A few minutes later, the back door to the truck opened and sunlight came piercing through the darkness. I had to squint to see clearly, but I noticed Brad was asleep.

'Wake up,' Angel said from outside the truck.

Brad took his time in waking up as Angel kept poking him with the butt of a rifle. Finally, he did wake up, cursing.

Brad got out of the truck first and I followed. I was so happy knowing that I was almost home.

That happiness was short lived when I got out of the truck and realised I wasn't home. I had been set up. Angel had some sick scheme planned out for us, and we walked right into it.

The truck stopped in the centre of a dirt road, sealing it shut. There was a small circular plain filled with nothing but thick grass, about knee-high, and trees around the circle for as far as I could see.

'What the fuck is this?' Brad asked Angel.

Angel smiled, the smile he would show off when he was up to no good, and said, 'This is as far as I go.'

'Where the hell are we?' I asked.

'You're close to where you need to be. Now stop asking questions and listen to me.' Angel urged, 'Run into the forest. There will be a plane waiting for you.'

'Bullshit!' Brad said.

'Do it. Did I not keep my word when I gave you that feast that your friend asked me to? I give you my word . . . There will be a plane coming to take you home.'

'Home,' Brad said, looking towards me.

'Home,' I reiterated.

Brad took off into the woods and left me standing there with Angel. I turned around quickly and tried to follow Brad. I kept up for a few seconds, but Brad was always so hyper and energetic. He ran fast, faster than I could ever imagine a human being running.

I lost him a while later and began walking at my own pace. I stopped every now and again to yell his name, but I was answered only by the cawing of crows.

I kept going deeper and deeper into the jungle. I had taken so many turns that I didn't even know where I was anymore. I tried to apply the strategy I had applied in the desert. Keep heading in one direction as compared to circles. It was a lot harder in the daytime. Every time I looked up at the sun, the glint caused my eyes to black out. I'd end up bumping into a tree or tripping on a log most of the time.

I decided it was just best to keep walking. With each step, I cursed Brad for running off the way he did. Angel never said anything about it being a race. We could have worked together and made it out of this mess. He chose to do this on his own. Or maybe he was just excited to get back home and thought I would slow him down?

I thought long and hard as to where he might be, and what I would do if I were him. Nothing came to mind for a long while. The sweat was trickling down my face and heat was escaping from the ground and going upwards, not making matters any easier.

I looked up, and the sun was no longer looming overhead. Night was coming, and if I had any chance of making it out of there, I had to give up on looking for Brad and just make do with what I had.

There was still light coming from somewhere beyond the trees. The sun hadn't gone down completely, but I didn't have much time. I started walking quicker, but the ground was so mucky that my feet were getting stuck.

*Muck!*

The ground couldn't be sticky unless there was water nearby. I was close to the end of this horrible jungle. I could feel it in my bones.

I kept following the muddy ground, turning around when it got more solid. If the ground was wet that meant that there must've been a stream or a lake or something that I could use to navigate, a place to set camp if nothing else.

Eventually I did stumble upon what I was looking for, quite literally, to my dismay.

I tripped on the root of a tree that had come jutting out of the soil and fell face first into a thin stream of water. I laughed and got to my feet. I looked up at the sky and thanked the heavens, if there was such a thing, and also made note that night was quickly approaching. I followed the stream, and soon it became thicker and deeper. It ran through trees for the most part, but after a certain point, it got so thick and deep that it had cleared whatever trees were around it. It was a full-fledged river. Trees were around its banks but nothing in its path. I knew that this would be the way out. *Rivers flow into oceans and seas and sometimes there are beaches, that's where the plane will be waiting for me!*

It was hopeful, but I was already running on fumes. I'd take whatever little I could get. I jumped into the river and was now knee-deep in water. I navigated my way through it, and soon my job became a lot easier when the current got stronger. All I had to do was let my body loose for a second and the current would take me away, closer to my goal. As soothing as that was, getting back to my feet and regaining control took up a lot of my energy. I got out of the river and found a nice spot along one of the banks to stop and breathe for a moment. Upon exiting, I took a little water in the palms of my hands and splashed my face and then drank a few sips. I was starting to feel pretty good about my chances of making it out of there. I had found the way. I looked back to see how much ground I had covered and thought about taking a break. I had no idea how to decipher that because beyond the river there were just miles and miles of trees, each tree no different than the next.

In the distance, through an opening in a narrow clearing, I spotted a thin trail of smoke.

'Brad!' I yelled.

It was useless. The smoke was too far away for my voice to travel. My impulses told me to double back and go get Brad, but I thought better of it. I would instead go to the end of this river, follow it back to the smoke, and get Brad. If this river was a dead end, I didn't want to waste valuable time. Brad must have taken a break from a path he found to set up camp.

I jumped back into the river and let the current take me to the ocean. After a while of fighting the current, I found it getting stronger and harder to fight. Regaining control had become a task. But I could hear where the river was flowing. There was splashing, beyond the splashes I was creating when fighting for control. The Ocean. It was close. I got out of the river and walked along the sides of the river. I walked for a while before stopping. The river had ended, and it did pour into an ocean. I wasn't relieved or happy to have found out about it, however. The ocean was several hundred feet below. I was standing at the foot of the river staring down a huge cliff. I hadn't realised before this moment how much I actually hated waterfalls, especially ones with a huge bed of sharp rocks at the end.

I had nothing.

In complete dismay, I turned around to walk back to where the smoke was coming out of, to look for Brad.

The thin trail of smoke that I had once seen was now thickening and darkening.

I had very little energy left in my body, but I managed to sprint towards its origins. The closer I got to the smoke, the more I realised how serious it was. It wasn't just a campfire, it was a full-fledged forest fire. If Brad was the one that started it, I might be able to catch up to him and we could help each other escape it.

I ran, and when I got tired, I ran some more. I kept going until I got to the fire. I hadn't taken any foolish turns, so I knew how to get back to the river. I knew I could survive the fire by staying in the water. I kept pushing on. Brad would have done the same for me. *I hope.*

When I had reached my destination, I realised I was right back where we started, in the plains, where Angel had left us. The dirt road was sealed off by fire.

'That son of a bitch!' I said out loud. He set the fire so that we would have no escape. He gave us his word that there would be a plane coming to take us home, but there was none. Instead he sealed us off. There was no escaping this fire. He left us here to die.

I saw the fire twirling, cracking down trees and sending up clouds of black smoke into the sky. I noticed that I would be surrounded by flames if I had stayed there any longer than I already had. I thought of going back in the direction that I came in, but it was too late. The fire had gotten to it. I was now in the centre of a circle of fire. In the distance, I noticed a small clearing where the fire hadn't gotten to yet. I ran through it, and a wall of fire sealed it shut behind me. *Close call, but I'm far from in the clear.* I stood back and watched the fire for a while, studying it. Analysing its behaviour and trying to figure something out, I had no idea what I was looking for but I studied it nonetheless. The longer I stuck around, the more steps back I had to take. The fire kept drawing closer towards me. It was sending me deeper and deeper into the forest. That's what Angel wanted. Eventually the fire would consume the whole place and there would be nowhere left to go. Instinctively, I almost sat there and admitted defeat. I would have waited for the fire to consume me if I hadn't realised something. 'The River!' I yelled. I darted towards it. I had no idea what I would do once I had gotten there, but I did know that water is effective against fires. It was my only hope.

A mile or so of running later, I realised that the fire was spreading equally in all directions. If I kept going, I would be in between the starting point of one fire and the ending point of another. I wouldn't make it to the river. I would be trapped and barbequed before I even got halfway. I had to think of something else.

I stopped and waited thinking of things to do. The fire didn't show me pity and kept coming towards me. When the fire came near me, I picked up a branch of a tree that had fallen by my feet and hurled it at the fire. It fell close to it and caught fire.

It was that barbarian act that had given me everything I needed. When the bark caught fire, it fell down in front of the reach of the forest fire and managed to somehow lodge itself in the ground and stand upright.

When it did, the flame that was on the tip of the branch was swaying towards the already raging forest fire.

I ran in the opposite direction and got a bigger piece of wood; it was part of a bark of a tree, heavy and long but still light enough to carry over my shoulder. I picked it up and took it back to the fire and set the tip of it ablaze. I ran towards where I got the piece of wood from and used it to set a whole line of trees on fire. I had created a fire in between the already existing and myself; I hoped that I was right in thinking what I was.

The old fire would come towards the new one that I had created, and the new one would be forced into the path of the old one because of the wind and pressure. It was scientific; it was sheer physics, and with a bit of luck, it would work out the way I planned—When the two fires met, there would be nothing left to burn and I will have found the one spot of land that would be unscathed by both fires, the one piece of land behind my line of fire and Angels. I would once again defeat all odds and survive. Right now, all I had to do was wait for the fire to kill everything in its path, including Brad.

There was a small possibility that Brad had thought of the same idea that I had and created his own safety net, but the odds of that were slim. It wasn't my idea to run off in different directions. Brad made that call all on his own. He took off without me. He could have been here with me if he hadn't been so stupid and impulsive. Did he deserve to die for that impulsive decision? No. But there was nothing that I could do about it. I was in the same situation as he was every single time. I managed to fight it one way or another. I managed to survive against all odds. I asked myself the same question once again: *Did Brad deserve to die?*

I was unsure of the answer, but I was sure of one thing. I deserved to live.

I watched as the fires met and destroyed everything in their paths. I was standing on the one piece of land that wasn't affected by the fire. I had sent the fire off to burn out in different directions, directions that were all away from my spot of safety.

I waited for the fires to die down, for the path to clear so that I could get out of there, find Angel, and kill him. I would probably never see him again; he was too smart to not think of me surviving. But I had given up all hope of ever getting home; I had given up all hope of ever seeing Jenna again.

When I thought everything was lost, I looked back at what I had learnt that day. I learnt that you could kill a fire using fire; I learnt that Brad needed to be put on a leash at all times and that Angel always . . . Always, kept his word.

A plane flew over my head and towards the centre of the field.

I couldn't believe it. He actually came through with the plane! I ran towards it waving up and down while it landed. I knew the pilot couldn't see me, but I didn't care. I had found the one thing that I had lost, the one thing I said I would never lose. I found hope again.

I got to the plane after what felt like running for hours. I stood outside it, as happy as a kid with a lollipop, and waited for it to open. It did. I got inside and took a seat.

Then I saw her.

The same woman who was in the back of the truck with us that night we ate dog meat. The same deep eyes and she was wearing the same robes as earlier, and her thick black hair was left open.

My jaw dropped as the door of the plane shut behind me. 'You!' I exclaimed. 'What are you doing here?'

# FIFTEEN

## ALL IS LOST

'Now is not the time to answer your questions,' she said, turning her back towards me. The pilot of the plane was sitting next to her; he was wearing the same outfits that Angel's mercenaries were wearing. I thought about the web of conspiracies that built up to this moment. Angel must have been in on this whole thing. He must have been the one that devised it.

'I understand that there is much that needs to be explained,' she said, not turning around to face me. 'But there is a time and a place for this. You will be taken home. That was the deal. Once you have reached your destination, everything will be explained to you.'

'You worked with Angel to see this whole thing through?' I asked, trying to find some sense of closure.

'Like I said before . . .' she said as she picked up a water bottle and handed it to me, 'all your doubts will be answered at the right time. For now, however, you must be tired and thirsty. Drink this.'

She handed the flask to me, and out of sheer thirst, I drank whatever was inside without question. That burning sensation and that uncomfortable numbness I had experienced at the feast overpowered everything else that I was feeling. I would have had the urge to fight the effects of the drink, but she was right: I was tired. Eventually I gave in and fell asleep.

I woke up when the plane landed. I didn't get to enjoy the plane ride because I was knocked out against my will.

'Get out,' the woman said, climbing out of the plane and onto the ground. I did as she asked.

When I put my feet on the ground, I felt a nice cool breeze blow into my hair. I could smell something familiar. It smelled like home. I was finally in Toronto. I knew just by the feeling of the air that I was close to home. At first I thought that I was in an airport because it was the obvious place to land a plane, but then I got out of the plane and noticed that I was on a stretch of road that I had never seen before covered in thick grass and tall trees. I was on the countryside, still somewhere close to home. There was a car waiting for the woman and me. I got into it shortly after she did. It was a white sedan. I noticed that the driver was one of Angel's men too. He had the same outfit on as the rest of them. *He wasn't kidding when he said his men were everywhere.*

'We know where you live. It isn't far from here,' she said to me.

'What's your name? Why are you doing this?' I questioned.

She smiled at me and looked deep into my eyes. 'In good time, Oliver. In good time,' she said.

I knew better than to get on Angel's bad side, so I thought it would probably be wisest to not mess with the woman he had sent out to finish the task he started, but I still had one more question to ask, something that had slipped my mind completely, and shouldn't have.

'Where's Brad?'

The woman turned to me surprised and shook her head from left to right. 'He didn't make it out of the forest.'

I looked down at my feet. I should have felt sadder than I was, but I thought that the only reason that I didn't was because I had already come to terms with the fact that Brad had already chosen his own fate.

I was trying to divert my attention from the subject, so I just peered out of the window of the moving car. I saw Maple leaves on the ground, wide roads and apartment buildings along them. I saw houses and homes and cars and kids playing on the streets. I knew I was close to home, close to Jenna.

I waited patiently as the streets got more and more familiar. Then I started instructing the driver as to which turns he needed to take. He assured me he knew where he was going, but it felt so great to finally know where I was that I couldn't help myself. The woman by my side who refused to divulge any information was rather amused with my child-like behaviour. I could swear that if a third person was looking at me and had known what I had been through to get to this stage, they wouldn't believe that I had seen half of the things that I had. It was all worth it; it was all forgotten. The thoughts I had about what normal was and wasn't, the debates I had in my head about whether or not I could go back to living without thinking of death, the doubts of what life would be like . . . they were all cleared. I knew that I was a few turns away from my driveway; I was a few steps away from the door of my house, a few inches away from Jenna's arms—a few inches away from everything that I've fought so hard to achieve.

When I did arrive at my driveway, I jumped out of the back seat of the car. I didn't wait for the driver to open the door. I didn't wait for the woman besides me to get out. I just darted for the front steps where my father was sitting with someone. I didn't bother to pay much attention to who he was sitting with because I was overjoyed to see him alive and healthy.

'Dad!' I said running towards him. He smiled and hugged me. He didn't say anything to me.

The woman came from behind me and nodded at my father. He nodded back.

'Wait. You know her?' I asked my father surprised.

My father didn't say anything to me. He just looked into the eyes of the woman behind me. I was stunned for a minute, and I didn't know what to make of this whole mess, but I would be damned if I didn't get any answers.

'What the hell . . .' I began to say but was cut off.

I felt an arm on my shoulder. I turned around and noticed it was Oliver, the bellboy from the UTT, the young security kid that would say hi to me each day as I went to work. I was so not used to seeing familiar faces that I didn't know how to react to his.

'It's probably best if you see for yourself what's changed since you've been gone,' he said to me as he took my hand and took me into the house.

I walked in the front door not sure what I had witnessed but sure of what I would do when I saw Jenna.

There she was, wearing a black dress, staring straight at me with tears in her eyes. She looked so beautiful but so sad.

She wasn't alone. My mother was next to her, holding her shoulder. My mother was sad too. I didn't say anything as I walked into the living room and noticed it was full of people that I had known and loved, some strangers, and some acquaintances.

I walked to the centre of the room and noticed that there was a casket in the middle of the room. If I was confused before, now I was just baffled.

'What's going on, Jenna?' I asked.

Jenna didn't respond, instead she began sobbing uncontrollably on my mother's shoulder.

I looked into the casket, and I was surprised at what I discovered.

A man in a suit, clean as a whistle but pale. The blood rushed from his face. His arms were crossed, folded, over his chest. I took a closer look and noticed that I wasn't just standing over a coffin looking at some stranger.

I was standing over my own coffin. I was in it.

# SIXTEEN

## RING A BELL?

I took a few steps back. I didn't know what to make of any of this.

'Come with me,' Oliver said to me as he dragged me out of the house.

I don't remember taking the steps out of the house. I remembered looking at Jenna and my mother, crying. I remembered looking around the house to see people staring at my dead body. If I was really dead, how could I have witnessed all this? Were the past few days just a lie? I had been told the whole time that now was not the time for questions, but I was certain that now was the time that they needed answering.

I walked up to where my father and the woman were standing and asked, 'What the hell is going on?'

'Son . . .' my dad said, but the woman cut him off.

'Oliver . . . My name is Angel,' she said.

I was quite confused, and I think it was showing on my face because she felt the need to elucidate and said, 'There isn't just one Angel. There are many of us. We preserve nature's way. When something dies, we see to it that the soul gets to where it needs to go.'

She paused looking over at me as if I was supposed to understand something.

My father knew that I hadn't grasped any of the information given to me, so he said, 'Son . . . Think about it for a second. Angel . . . Angel of death.'

Suddenly, it made a little sense to me. Some psychopath wasn't toying with me; my soul was being set free by one of the many Grim Reapers.

*Okay, even thinking about it sounds silly.*

'What the hell are you trying to say?' I asked.

Oliver, the security kid, came up next to me and said, 'I'll try to make this as clear to you as I possibly can. This may come as bit of a shock to you, but no one else in the living world could see me other than you.'

The whole concept sounded alien to me, but I decided to try and piece it together anyway.

At the lobby of the UTT, Oliver would always say hi to me, and I would always have a conversation with him but no one would even acknowledge him. No one even spoke about him at the office. During the fire drills, when everyone was waiting for instructions, no one would pay attention to what Oliver was doing. They would wait for the big guy to come around and give instructions. He wasn't real. I was the only one that could see him; I was the only one that could talk to him. *But why?*

'I'm your guardian angel. I am sent to people that are set to die soon, you know to make sure things are in order for the Angels,' he said Angel the same way that Angel had said it the first time—*Aa-Ni-Yell.*

'What about Becky, Francine, Brad, and Mister Astiff? Did they have guardian angels too?' I asked.

'Probably,' he said. 'It's hard to know for sure. Some people meet theirs, others don't.'

'How did I . . .' I was about to ask a question, but I couldn't really put my finger on what it was exactly.

'How did you die?' Angel asked me. She looked at me concerned, as if I wasn't taking it as well as she'd hoped. She then looked over at Oliver who was standing next to me.

'Well, that day you came into work for that big meeting . . . you remember, right?'

How could I forget? It was the meeting that changed my life. I was in it one minute, and in a desert the next. I nodded.

Oliver acknowledged my nod and said, 'Well, think about what really happened that day. Think hard and think deep.'

I did as he asked; I replayed the whole instance in my mind.

I shut my eyes after I said this, trying to make sense of it all in my head.

*'No,' said Henry.*

*'No?' asked Mister Astiff. I noticed that our team had a smile on their faces. What I said didn't make sense to Henry and Mitch, but at least, the smile reassured me that it was better than anything Mister Astiff, Brad, and Francine could come up with.*

*'The product isn't ready yet. We can't serve it if it doesn't exist.'*

*Brad was getting impatient, the way he'd always get when he was made to sit for too long. He began to interrupt anything that anyone was saying. Henry and Mitch weren't fazed by this and went on dealing with the situation calmly. Their calmness was making Mister Astiff livid because he had no control over the matter, and he hated not being in control. Francine just sat there chewing her nails, and as for me, I was sitting there trying to shut out the mind-numbing ringing in my ear.*

*When the yelling was almost insufferable, Becky walked in.*

*'Not now, Becky!' Mister Astiff yelled.*

*'Mister Jacoby is on line two for you,' she said. 'He said it's urgent.'*

*The yelling didn't die down at all. Brad kept hurling ideas at Henry and Mitch, and the two of them were just shutting down everything that Brad threw at them. Francine sat there chewing her nails; Mister Astiff kept ignoring everything that Becky was saying and yelling at the two suited men in front of him. Becky kept cutting in reminding Mister Astiff that there was a call for him, but she remained ignored.*

*All this wasn't even half as painful as the ringing. Oh that damn ringing! I couldn't take it anymore. I shut my eyes and covered my face, until all that there was, was darkness and that painful ring, a ring so sharp and loud that it made my head rattle. I pressed my fingers into my eyes trying to feel something, anything but that incessant ringing. Finally, the ringing got so loud that it felt as though it couldn't get any louder.*

*Then it stopped.*

'There was a ringing in my ears,' I said. 'I shut my eyes, and when I opened them, I was in a desert!'

'Was the ringing just in your ears?' Oliver added.

I thought harder and deeper about the moment.

The ringing wasn't coming from inside my head. It was a ringing I was familiar with but not the same one that I had associated it with initially. It was the fire alarm at the UTT. A sound that I had become so used to hearing over the period of my first few days at UTT that I could have easily misplaced the thought of it with something else.

'There was a fire!' I exclaimed.

'An actual one this time,' my guardian angel said. 'The sixty-seventh and sixty-eighth floors were really under repairs for some damages. While repairing it, the electricians hit a cable and that cable caused a fire in the elevator shaft. It spread into the conference room of *The Trick of the Trade*.'

'I died in the fire?' I asked.

'Yes, along with Becky, Francine, Brad, and Robert,' he replied.

'There were others with us in the meeting, and others in the office at the time. Did they all die too?' I asked.

'No, they made it out of the building. Some people were injured but not killed in the fire. The other two people with you in the meeting, Mitch and Henry . . . they were in the hospital for a while, but they're okay now. Alive,' he answered.

'So if I was dead the whole time and Brad, Francine, Becky, and Mister Astiff were all dead too, how did they all die before my eyes?'

Angel walked up close to me and looked over at my father and then back at me. She then said, 'Oliver, we are not evil people . . . we are doing nature's will. When the soul needs to part with the body, it is an act that we cannot fight. All we do, as Angels, is buy time for the deceased, giving you a chance to live a little more before your soul finally dies.'

I looked over at my father who was standing there silent. 'Does this mean that you're dead too?' I asked him.

'I made a deal with Angel,' he said, pointing at the woman next to him. 'I said I would join them if they let me see you one more time.'

'Join them? You want to become one of the men who kills people?' I asked, appalled.

Angel came close to me and said, 'We do not kill people. You make us seem like heartless monsters. I told you already, we reap the souls of those that are already dead. Imagine if no one came to find you in that desert where you woke up and you were left wandering it for all eternity. We gave you a chance to live, the make choices, to learn how to value what you had and cherish every memory.'

'Why was I given a chance to see all this? Why did you let the others get reaped but still keep me here to witness my own funeral?' I asked.

'They want you to join us, son,' my father said. 'Become a reaper. An Angel.'

All this was too much to take in. Did I really want to be one of them? Did I want to be the one that ends people's lives? Stare death in the face every day?

'You have a niceness in you, a purity that we seek out in all our reapers. You have the ability to not make rash decisions and let the souls choose their fate for themselves,' Angel said.

I thought about what Angel had done in the desert. He had used threats on us but never really acted on them. He had told us time and again that he would kill us but never killed us. He always gave us a choice. With the game he played with the gun, he gave us a chance to go in the order we wanted to. He gave two people a chance to go plant a bomb. He gave one person a choice as to what they wanted before they died. He gave Brad a chance to stay alive.

'This was all just a test?' I said, finally coming to some sense of clarity.

'We are constantly looking for more reapers among the souls that get sent to us.' She said to me, 'If they happen to come in large groups, we pick the finest of them to offer a position to.'

I looked over at my father who was standing there with a proud look on his face, 'You survived too?' I asked him.

He nodded.

Without thinking, I hugged him tight. I had witnessed the horrors that he had. I participated in a staring contest with the eyes of fear and came out victorious, and he had done the same.

When the hug was broken, I looked over at Angel. 'And if I agree, I get to make a demand of my choosing?'

'Anything that is within our limits,' she said.

I thought about it carefully for a second or two and then shook my head. 'I'll do it,' I said. 'I will become a reaper. But here is my stipulation—'

I paused for a while to see if there were any doubts. There were none, so I continued, 'When Jenna dies . . . I want to reap her soul in any way that I see fit. No questions asked.'

Angel nodded.

If there were anything to do this for, I would do it so that I could be with Jenna one more time, so that I could talk to her once again. Hold her in my arms, maybe; if I'm lucky, convince her to join me and be with me forever in the afterlife. I was given the greatest gift of all time yet again on my journeys: I was given hope.

'Welcome aboard, Oliver Turner,' Angel said as she walked to the car with my guardian angel. 'We'll meet again,' she said as she got in the car.

*My name is . . . was, was, Oliver Turner. But you can call me Angel.*